THE WAY HOME

by Lucenzo Guarino

COPYWRITE PAGE
Name: Guarino, Lucenzo-Author.
Title: The Way Home
Description:
Published in 2016

Summary: When Stella Johanson finds a cub Polar Bear in her backyard, she must keep it a secret from her family. Luckily for Stella, her grandpa Gustav is willing to help her hid Max along the way of their long journey to the northern tip of Sweden. The adventure and mayhem that encounters them is one for the record books.

Identifiers: LCCN (print) | ISBN) 978-0-9965618-3-9 | ISBN 10-: 0-9965618-3-8)
BISAC- JUV000000- Juvenile Fiction- General
BISAC- JUV002030- Juvenile Fiction- Animals-Bears

TABLE OF CONTENTS

Chapter One
Page 1
Chapter Two
Page 12
Chapter Three
Page 24
Chapter Four
Page 39
Chapter Five
Page 51
Chapter Six
Page 65
Chapter Seven
Page 76
Chapter Seven
Page 76
Chapter Eight
Page 86
Chapter Nine
Page 100
Chapter Ten
113
Chapter eleven
Page 128
Chapter tweleve
page 140
Chapter Thirteen
Page 152

Facts about Sweden
Page 166-167

Polar Bear
Page 168

Ice Hotel
Page 169

WWF
Page 170

Recipes
Pages 171-180

CHAPTER ONE

FARFAR'S STORY

"His eyes were fierce and as black as coals. They gleamed like onyx stones peering out of the snow-covered expanse. I slid closer to him, and our eyes locked. I bent down and tried to unfasten my skis, but I was shivering too much. Not with cold, but with fear..."

"*You* scared Farfar? I don't believe that," interrupted Stella, her bright blue eyes twinkling with anticipation.

"Of course, I was," replied Gustav, Stella's grandpa, "Leo was only a cub then, but he looked fierce enough to me. His white furry frame stood frozen on the spot glaring at me, watching every move I made."

Stella was lying flat on her stomach, sprawled across the sitting room rug, her pointed chin resting in the palms of her hands. Her nose twitched nervously as she listened to her grandpa's story.

She had heard the tale of his encounter with Leo the Polar bear many times before. Nonetheless, she never tired of listening to how her grandpa had freed the cub from the trap.

"How did you know his name was Leo?"

Stella always asked loads of questions, and grandpa had an answer to every one of them.

"Well, I didn't at the time, but Leo seemed to fit him perfectly."

Gustav, who was sitting in his well-used armchair leant closer to Stella. His watery blue eyes stared into his granddaughter's. Stella sat up, crossed her legs, and pushed her long blond hair behind her small pixie ears. She waited-eyes wide and lips pursed. "I trod knee deep in the snow towards Leo, still trembling like a leaf. That's when I noticed that the pure white fur on his paw was dark red. Poor Leo's paw was clamped in a trap and he was bleeding. There was no time to lose. I couldn't leave him there, an easy prey for scavengers. I plodded nearer to him as cautiously as I could. Which wasn't easy in all that snow."

"Grrr!" growled Gustav making Stella jump in fright. A black glossy head that had been resting peacefully on her knees shot up and pricked up its ears in alarm. Stella stroked the soft silky head of her Cocker Spaniel, both to soothe her own fear and to reassure her pet. Sofi made a funny sighing noise and happily settled down again, resting her chin on her mistress' lap.

"Leo growled at me, his eyes brilliant and determined. Let me tell you, that little bear had a lot of courage. It reminds me of a little girl I know," added Gustav winking at Stella.

Stella swallowed hard and gripped her knees tightly. "But how did you open the trap without him biting you?"

"I stared straight into Leo's jet-black eyes, and something happened between us. We connected like two blood brothers.

He knew he could trust me and that I was there to save him. Polar bears are intelligent animals you know. They can sense if you are good or bad."

Gustav settled back in his armchair again. His eyes wandered past Stella, as his thoughts travelled back into the past.

"Leo eyed me closely but uttered not one more growl. I knelt with caution and pulled hard on the trap, and he was free. Our eyes met again, his were ablaze with life and in those few seconds our friendship was sealed. Then with a flash he bounded away into the wild winter landscape, tripping over his injured paw as he went. I stood there in awe watching the beautiful wild animal, deep down hoping he would turn back. But the cuddly mass of white fur was soon swallowed up by the icy expanse of the Lapland."

"But why didn't you take him home to the stuga and bandage him?" said Stella, her light eyebrows scrunching up.

"Because Leo didn't belong to me. He belonged to his mother and father. They would soon find him again and take care of his injured paw. Leo and I will always be friends but he belongs to the wild."

Stella shook her white-blond hair unable to mask her disapproval. She was not sure Leo's mother had ever found him. She was worried that Leo had not survived at all. But she would not tell her grandpa that. It would upset him.

"Come on you two," interrupted a gentle but firm voice from the open door leading to the kitchen.

Emma, Stella's mother walked into the living room wiping her hands on the blue and green Pippi Longstocking apron dress, Stella had made for Mother's Day.

She slipped her arms under Stella's and heaved her up from the rug, then wrapped her arms around her daughter. Sofi gingerly stood up on her paws and shook her body vigorously from head to tail. Then looked up at Emma with her sulky dark eyes gleaming behind long black lashes.

Emma's eyes were as bright blue as her daughter's, and her long blond hair was tied in a neat plait that trailed along her back.

"Your stories go on and on pappa. You'd be here until midnight if we didn't stop you, " Emma reprimanded Gustav, shaking her head.

"Stella it's already past your bedtime. Tomorrow is a special day and you need all the rest you can get."

Stella's tummy rumbled at the thought. Yes, tomorrow was a special day indeed, but a scary one too. She was going to play at the most famous opera house in Stockholm, the 'Kungliga Operan'. Both her father and her grandpa Gustav had played there before her, many years ago.

Stella could picture the high arched ceilings painted white and decorated with rich golden twirls and whirls, bordered with magnificent paintings of angels and veiled beauties. But what was breathtaking, were the smells and sounds. The scent of the wax they used to polish the marble floors and the sounds of the instruments as they tuned up before the concert.

Stella thought of her own violin, the one she had received for her tenth birthday. It was a full-size violin, and she could manage it perfectly now. The violin had belonged to her father Alexander and was a very precious instrument.

Her father rarely played the violin anymore, Stella thought sadly. But she would play and play, until one day, she would become so good the Gothenburg Opera house would invite her to play for them. That was Stella's dream. To become a leading violinist for the Gothenburg symphony orchestra and play for the most amazing opera house in Sweden.

Her frail shoulders shuddered at the thought of tomorrow night and the wonders of the opera house. Sofi licked Stella's hand and wagged her tail as if acknowledging the little girl's apprehension. Stella beamed at her pet and bent down to scoop the animal up into her arms. Sofi was no longer a pup, but Stella could carry her without much difficulty.

She cuddled Sofi and looked over at her dad, who was sitting on the divan watching his favorite program. Ice hockey. He loved ice hockey and was a great fan of the Stockholm team. There was just one funny twist about pappa. He could hardly even stand up straight on skates. But he was an excellent cross-country skier.

"Pappa, are you sure I'll be good enough at the concert?" asked Stella, as she jumped into her dad's lap with Sofi, blocking his view of the match. He tore his gaze from the exciting event, blinked twice, and beamed at Stella.

"You'll be the best! The most enchanting, the

loveliest and sweetest violinist ever to set foot in the Kungliga Operan. People will whisper, 'look that is the Alexander Johansson's daughter, the one with magic in her fingers and sparks in her bow.' You'll enchant the audience they will acclaim 'encore! Encore Stella!'"

Stella arched her eyebrows and shook her golden head. "Pappa, you have more imagination than Farfar."

Her father opened his arms-palms up and lifted his shoulders. "It can't be helped if you're the best, the star of the show. That's why we called you 'Stella' our little music star."

"Enough you two," interrupted Emma again. "I wonder why the men in this family aren't famous novelists?"

Stella giggled and jumped up, dropping Sofi on the sofa next to her father. She reached over her pet to kiss her father goodnight. "God natt pappa," she whispered her blue eyes gleaming. "I'll make sparks fly from my bow like a witch from her wand."

"You do that my bright little star, show them you're a Johansson kid!" Alexander then turned his gaze back to the screen, where the yellow, red and blue players of the Djurgarden Stockholm team swished gracefully over the

ice.
Stella hugged her grandpa goodnight. The rough fabric of his favorite grey roll necked jumper scratched on her soft cheek, and a faint whiff of tobacco tickled her nostrils.
She knew he had the bad habit of consuming the popular Swedish tobacco, 'Snus'. She thought he looked comical when he slipped the small piece of tobacco under his upper lip. It reminded Stella of a miniature teabag and made his lip bulge slightly.

"You'll be there won't you Farfar," she whispered in his ear, her voice trembling.

"I wouldn't miss your first big night for anything in the world," he replied squeezing Stella's slight frame, sending a wave of warmth and renewed courage through her whole being.

Stella nodded, then, with Sofi at her heels, she headed for the stairs leading up to her bedroom. Little did the two friends know that they would not be getting much sleep that night.

Chapter Glossary

Farfar [f'ar:far] - Grandpa

Pappa [p'ap:a] - dad

Stuga [st'u:ga] - Typical summer house or holiday home

God natt pappa [go:d nat: p'ap:a] - Goodnight dad

Kungliga Operan: The Royal Swedish Opera in Stockholm. Music, ballet and plays are carried out in this famous Swedish venue.

Gothenburg Opera house: The Famous opera house in Gothenburg, built in a modern style.

Chapter Questions

1. Who did Leo remind Gustav of and why?
2. How did Sophia receive her violin?
3. What was Stella's dream?
4. What did Stella fear about Leo?

C

H

A

P

T

E

R

T

W

O

STELLA FINDS MAX

Emma sat on Stella's bed and tucked her in while Sofi curled up in a ball and snuggled up among the family of soft toys that crowded the duvet.

She then pushed her slight frame up from the bed with some effort and moved towards the window. She was about to draw the thick curtains over the cold winter night when Stella said.

"Please mamma, can you leave them open. I love to watch the snowflakes float down from the night sky, while

I'm warm and snuggled up in my bed."

Emma smiled at her daughter and thin lines of tiredness appeared around her eyes. Stella looked so small and vulnerable under her thickly padded cocoon. Emma came and knelt by Stella's bed and pulled her long plait over her shoulder. Then with the hair at the tip of her plait, she tickled Stella's nose.

"You'll be just fine," Emma said, stroking her daughter's hair and brushing her forehead with her lips. "Besides, there's a full moon shining tonight, and you're meant to sleep, not watch what's happening outside."

Stella pulled the duvet right up over her nose so that only her blue eyes were visible, reflecting her anxiety.

"If you go straight to sleep and play the way you always do at the concert, pappa has a fantastic surprise for you," added Emma her smile lighting up her worn face.

Stella sat up in bed again and opened her mouth ready to pester her mother with questions.

"Hush Stella, no more of your questions, get to sleep now. You'll just have to wait and see," said Emma pushing Stella back down and covering her right up to her chin with the soft duvet cover.

"Please mamma, can you give me a clue?" pressed

Stella.

"No clues now. Only sweet dreams," said Emma, an amused smile playing on her lips. She then turned off Stella's bedside light and gently closed the bedroom door behind her

Stella reached out for Pippi, who was always close at hand and tugged at the raggedy doll's red yarn pigtails in frustration.

"How can I sleep now Sofi?" she complained to her Cocker Spaniel, who was already half asleep, and barely picked up her left ear in response.

Stella tossed and turned and pulled at Pippi trying to figure out what the surprise could be. Finally, she gave up and thought of her grandpa freeing Leo from his trap.

She imagined him packing the cub into his backpack and sliding swiftly on his skis back to his stuga. At the hut, he would have bathe the polar bear's paw and bandaged it carefully. Once cured of his injury Leo and her grandpa would have had loads of fun sledging and playing in the snow.

Her eyelids grew heavier and heavier, and she finally drifted off to sleep.

"Grrr!"

Stella woke up with a start. Leo! She thought. It took her a few moments to remember where she was. Soft moonlight was filtering through the window, and she could see Sofi's silhouette, paws up on the windowsill peering out.

"Rrroof," barked Sofi under her breath.

"Shhh!" whispered Stella, surprised to hear her pet bark. Sofi never usually growled or barked, and if she did it was only when they played tug of war with her favorite soft toy rabbit. Sofi too had a passion for stuffed animals, especially rabbits.

Stella swung her legs over the side of the bed, pushed her duvet off, and slipped out of bed. The wooden floorboards felt cool under her bare feet as she walked over to the window and peered out.

The night was brilliant and clear, and the moonlight shone brightly over the snow-covered ground in the back garden. It was nearly as bright as the midnight sun up in the northern lands, where the sun never set during the summer months.

"What is it Sofi?" whispered Stella stroking the soft coat and patting her head. "I can't see anything weird out there."

Stella was not a sissy. She did not believe in monsters anymore. However, burglars were for real. Stella lived in a quiet area of Stockholm, and she had never heard of any break-ins in their neighborhood.

She pressed her nose and forehead against the cold window pane and cradled her eyes with her hands to get a better view. Nobody seemed to be lurking about in the garden. Everything was quiet.

Sofi, who was still up against the window ledge, now started scratching on the wood. "Grrrr." Her growl was low and continuous.

"There must be something out there in the garden," Stella murmured with a frown.

It was time for a little investigation. She would be able to spot any suspicious footprints in the snow, if there were any, and only then would she call for help and set Sofi on the thief's heels. If, of course, there was anybody out there in the first place.

Stella took Sofi by the scruff of the neck and pulled her off the windowsill. "Shh," she scolded again, "sit down, quiet now. We'll creep downstairs to see what's worrying you so much. But DON'T bark or we'll get into trouble."

Stella then slipped on her fleecy dressing gown that

was hanging on a peg behind the door next to Sofi's leash. She attached her pet to leash just in case she ran off. Sofi sometimes did run off, and then it was impossible to catch her.

She opened the bedroom door ever so quietly and peeped around the crack onto the landing. It was plunged into darkness. The landing had no windows to allow the moon rays to seep through, and she could hardly see anything.

Stella squeezed her eyes shut then opened them again. That was a bit better. Sofi tugged at the leash jerking Stella forward and out of the bedroom. In the dog's rush to get out Stella forgot to put on her slippers. She also had a troublesome time pulling at the leash to slow Sofi down and avoid tripping on the dark staircase.

'Click, click, click'. Sofi's pattering resounded on the steps and through the silent house. Stella hoped the noise would not wake anyone up. She held her breath until she reached the bottom step. Then, still tugged along by Sofi, she crossed the dining room and entered the kitchen.

The hum of the dishwasher and the green light of the freezer's temperature gauge gave the kitchen an eerie gloom. It flashed -17. Stella shivered, suddenly realizing she was still barefoot. The temperature outside would be freezing with the icy February snow covering the ground.

It was too late to go back upstairs, and Sofi was getting more and more eager to get out. She was now scratching on the kitchen door that led into the back garden.

Stella pulled hard at the leash again, then turned the latch to unlock it and pulled the door ajar. Icy fingers gripped at her bare feet and calves as the freezing night air whooshed through the crack of the open door.

Before she could change her mind and shut out the outside winter world, Sofi jerked hard and pulled the leash from Stella's hand, slipped through the crack and disappeared into the moonlit garden.

"Oh no," hissed Stella under her breath and followed her dog into the night.

The freezing snow pricked at the soles of Stella's bare feet, but she paid no attention, she was desperately searching for Sofi, who was nowhere to found.

The back garden was not very large. Just a rectangular patch of grass, with a small trampoline at the far end to the right of the garden shed. This was where Emma kept all her gardening tools, and Alexander stored the skis, ice skates and sledges.

Stella's eyes scanned the garden, the moonlight shedding spooky shadows on the snow. That was when she heard Sofi growl deeply again like distant rolling thunder. The sound was coming from behind the shed. Stella gingerly made her way towards it, her feet now burning from the icy snow. As she came closer to the shed, she saw Sofi's shadow on the snow, and next to hers was another, unfamiliar one. It was moving slowly and getting bigger and bigger, and it was coming towards her.

As the shadow grew, Stella started backing up towards the kitchen door. Then everything happened at once. Sofi barked and the huge shadow jumped out from behind the shed. Stella's mouth dropped open in horror and was about to let out a scream, when, instead, she giggled with glee and skipped towards the shed, just as Sofi jumped around the corner in pursuit of the mysterious shadow.

"Just look at him Sofi! I've never seen anything as cute as this little fellow in my whole life."

There, on the brilliant snow was a baby polar bear, as white as the ground he was sitting on. His brilliant black eyes were staring back at Stella's. He was shivering with fear as he tried to get up and jump away from her, but he was still a clumsy cub and fell flat on his chin.

"You poor helpless teddy bear," giggled Stella getting closer to him and reaching out to pat him. He drew his tiny ears back and growled softly. "Grrr," growled Sofi back, defending Sofi from the little beast.

"Stop that immediately you bad dog," scolded Stella frowning at Sofi, "you'll scare the poor baby bear."

Sofi pulled back her ears and sat down meekly, upset at Stella's reaction. The Polar bear may have been a baby, but he was nearly as big as Sofi, who did not look happy about the attention her mistress was giving the white ball of fur.

Meanwhile, Stella had managed to calm the cub and was stroking his thick fur. His ears straightened up and he sniffed the air around Stella's hand, then he licked it and sat down on the snow again.

"He adores me," said Stella delighted, "he thinks I'm his mother. I have to rescue him from the cold and take him to a safe shelter."

If Sofi could have lifted her eyebrows in exasperation she would have. But all she did was look up sulkily through her long black lashes and followed Stella sheepishly back into the warm house.

What Stella had not thought of was that Polar bears

are used to the cold. But she was now too intent on saving the little bear from the freezing night.

Somewhere in Stella's imaginative head, thoughts were swirling. A little voice was telling her that this was her chance to make up for the unfinished task her grandpa had left unsettled more than ten years ago. On that famous day on the Lapland, when he had left Leo to his fate.

Chapter Glossary

Midnight Summer Facts:

The farther you travel toward the north pole, the longer the days are in summer and the shorter they are in winter.

The Midnight Sun is the name given the sun when it can be seen at midnight during the Arctic or Antarctic summer. From March 21 to September 23, the sun is visible 24 hours a day at the North Pole. The midnight sun occurs because the earth's axis tilts toward the sun in summer and away from the sun in winter.

Chapter Questions

1. What did Stella first think was the noise outside?
2. What was the main reasoning behind Stella taking the pup out of the cold?

CHAPTER THREE

STELLA HIDES MAX

Stella's eyes fluttered open. She was startled by a sticky, icky feeling on her cheek. She brought her hand up to her face and felt warm soft fur. It was Sofi waking her up, reminding her it was pee time.

"I'm SOOO tired," she groaned then yawned loudly. "Can't you let yourself out this morning Sofi? I must have had a bad dream. I remember we went out in the icy cold and..."

Stella sat up with a start knocking Sofi's paws off the bed. It had not been a bad dream at all. They *had* ventured out in the cold last night, Sofi had heard something in the garden.

"Of course, The polar bear cub," she exclaimed. Stella scanned the bedroom frantically searching for the little bear. Next, she jumped out of bed, lifted the duvet cover and looked under the bed. Nothing, only **Klappa**, her black plush toy horse. She looked behind the laundry basket and under her desk, then went over to her wardrobe, where the door stood ajar. The cub was nowhere to be seen.

Stella remembered creeping upstairs with the cub in her arms. Her fingers and toes crossed hoping no one would hear them. She had gently eased him on the bed where he had settled among her soft toys burrowing his nose under one of her **mumintrolls** and had soon fallen fast asleep.

Stella stopped in her tracks. The bed! She spun around to look at the jumble of bed clothes and toys. Sofi was now sitting on it, her silky black head resting on her paws. Her large soft black eyes following Stella's movements. Stella searched the bed. It took her a while before she spotted the bear, cradled between her white **Mumintroll** and **Pippi Longstocking.** The little bear looked just like one of her other cuddly toys. One of the bigger ones of course. His soft white fur was such a contrast with Sofi's black glossy coat.

"It wasn't a dream Sofi," said Stella beaming, "the little bear is real."

Stella knelt beside the bed resting her elbows on the duvet, her chin cradled in her hands, staring in awe at the sleeping cub. Sofi's head was resting on her paws again. She lifted one eyebrow then the other as she watched her mistress with gloomy eyes. Stella had forgotten all about pee time, in fact, she had hardly given Sofi a second thought.

"I wonder if it's a boy or a girl?" mused Stella. "I bet you it's a boy, like Farfar's friend Leo."

The little bear's big tummy rose and fell. His black nose twitched and one of his paws shuddered slightly.

"I have to find a name for him, how about Snowball? No, that's too obvious and babyish. I know! Lars, like the little polar bear in those books mamma used to read every night before she got ill and couldn't read to me anymore."

Stella swallowed down a lump in her throat. She used to love it when her mamma read to her. But a few years ago, the doctors told pappa that mamma was sick. Not terribly sick, not extremely dangerously sick, but enough to be very, very tired. That was when Farfar had come to live with them, to help look after Stella. He was the one who told Stella stories now. But Farfar did not need books. His stories jumped out of his head and came to life. Just like those wild animals Stella had seen with pappa at the Museum of Natural History. Stella had marveled at how real those wild animals looked on the gigantic 3D screen in the I-Max theatre.

She remembered she had seen a film on polar bears and whales. Never in her most secret dreams would she have imagined that one of those animals would come out of the screen and land in their back garden.

"Yes! That's what I'll call him. I just know it's a boy. Max. That's where I first saw him, on the I-Max screen."

Stella beamed happily, like Farfar, she knew the name was just right.

The mattress bounced up and down as Sofi jumped off the bed and sat in front of the door. She turned her head looking eagerly at Stella and wagged her tail. It thudded loudly against the door.

"Thump, thump thump." Stella hadn't even noticed her pet was no longer on the bed. She was staring intently at the little bear, who was now stirring. Max opened his mouth wide to yawn, and his pink tongue rolled out. He then stretched his paws, opened his little black eyes, and blinked twice.

"Hey, Max. Welcome to your new home," said Stella, tickling his tummy with her fingers as he rolled over on to 'Peo Teddy' whose ribbon and left ear were tattered from years of use. Max blinked again and sniffed her hand. He then started to lick Stella's hand, with long and warm strokes.

"You must be hungry poor little bear," she exclaimed, realizing that she had no idea what baby polar bears ate.

"He might like your dog biscuits," pondered Stella, finally looking over at Sofi, who whipped her tail even more eagerly now that her mistress had noticed her.

Sofi would not have wagged her tail at all had she known that Stella was about to give her biscuits away. All Sofi was worried about now was that, if she didn't go out soon she would wee right on the floor. Then they would both get into trouble.

"Hmm," mumbled Stella again. "Maybe I should look for some milk too. I wonder how I'm going to give that to you. There aren't any baby bottles around the house anymore."

Max was now chewing and pawing at Pippi's red hair. Stella would use the opportunity to leave him a few minutes and slip quietly down to the kitchen to see what she could find. She also had to let Sofi out, who was now desperately scratching at the bedroom door.

Stella often woke up earlier than anyone else in the house, because of Sofi. But this morning it was later than usual, and she could hear her father in the bathroom having his shower. She had to be quick before anyone noticed what she was up to.

No one was downstairs yet. Her mother was probably still sleeping. Stella was sure she was trying to get as much rest as possible, to be at her best for Stella's performance.

Farfar was not up yet. He usually took his time in the mornings, although he insisted his sleep was not the same now that he was an old man.

Stella let Sofi out from the kitchen door. She then started rummaging in the fridge. She took out a carton of milk and poured some into a mug. Then on second thoughts, decided to keep the carton, and hid it under her dressing gown, not without some difficulty. Next, she opened the cupboard under the sink and found the packet of dog biscuits she was looking for. She stuffed two large handfuls of biscuits in her pockets, then quickly put the pack away again.

She looked around the kitchen, thinking what else she might need for Max. Her stomach started to grumble.

"I can't have my breakfast yet, we've got to feed Max first," she whispered to Sofi. Stella then realized her pet was still outside.

She let Sofi in and hushed her eager sniffs and snorts as she jumped up and tried to get her nose into Stella's pockets.

"Quiet, you naughty dog. You'll get us into trouble." Stella pushed Sofi down and made her way back upstairs as quietly as she could with Sofi pattering behind.

Stella heard the water gushing in the shower. Pappa always took his time to get ready for work in the mornings, she thought. Then she quickly slipped back into her room, closed the door, and sighed with relief. Max had fallen asleep again, his black nose buried in Pippi's bright red hair.

"How much does he sleep?" whispered Stella in surprise. By now she was itching to feed and play with her new pet.

There was a soft knock at the door. Stella jumped up in fright. She quickly hid the carton of milk under the bed and threw the duvet over Max.

Alexander popped his head round the door, and before he could come in Stella rushed up to him and reached up to give him a kiss.

"You're already up my little star," whispered Alexander not wanting to disturb his sleeping wife. "Remember to be ready by six tonight. I'm treating everyone to a very special dinner in a secret place. But don't tell anyone." Stella would usually have flooded her father with questions, but she was too worried he would spot Max sleeping under the duvet, so she nodded eagerly and replied, "Yes pappa, I'll be super ready, Farfar will love it too. I just hope mamma will be OK."

Stella's eyes met her father's. She caught a flicker of sadness in them despite his cheerful smile. But she could see right into his head. Stella knew how worried her father was about her mother's health.

Farfar, on the other hand, was something else. You could never tell what he had on his mind. He was always full of surprises. Stella never knew what he would come up with next.

When her father kissed her quickly on the forehead, Stella realised the dinner treat was probably the surprise her mother had hinted at last night. She would have loved to press him about it, but she wanted him to leave as quickly as possible.

The second the door closed behind him a funny noise rose from under the bed clothes. It sounded like a stifled crowing. Stella saw the cover move, and Sofi growled.

"Oh, stop it Sofi. It's Max of course, he's woken up. Poor little bear, now he must really be starving!"

She lifted the duvet and sure enough there was Max rolled over on his back looking up at her. His bright black eyes stared back at her. He opened his mouth, stuck out his tongue and yawned, shook his head and fluffy white body, then toppled over onto his tummy legs spread out wide.

Stella giggled at the sight. "He's so clumsy and adorable! Come here my little bear," she said picking him up and cuddling Max against her cheek. His fur was softer than any in her enormous collection. Stella cradled him in her neck, and he sniffed around under her hair and licked her ear.

Stella chuckled with delight. She gently grasped around him with both her hands to pull him away from her. It felt as if she had plunged her hands deep into cotton wool. As she drew him away to put him on the wooden floor beside her bed, his claws got tangled in her hair. Stella was amazed at the size of his paws and the length of his claws.

Max was hilariously clumsy. He gingerly pushed himself up on his forepaws and wobbled unsteadily, his hind paws trailing behind. He tilted his head and sniffed the air around him. She watched in awe as he padded and toppled around, slipping on the polished floorboards. He was finding it hard to get a firm grip on the surface. He managed to reach Sofi, who compared to him was as black as coal, and quite big. His small ears perked up and his black nose twitched, smelling out his new surroundings. Sofi sat up and eyed him suspiciously.

"Time for breakfast," announced Stella, looking forward to the new experience of feeding a real to life Polar Bear.

Sofi did not look happy when Stella took her water bowl and emptied it in the aloe vera plant pot she kept on the windowsill. Stella stretched her arm under her bed and reached for the carton of milk, then poured some into the bowl. She picked Max up and sat down with him cradled in her lap. She dipped the spoon in the milk and poured a little into Max's mouth.

He immediately started licking around his mouth and the spoon, his pink tongue moving fast and eagerly. Stella realized that he could probably lap up the milk by himself. She put him down next to the bowl and he clumsily plunged his nose right in the milk.

"Tchiii," sneezed Max, toppling over. Stella laughed out loud. Max was so comical and adorable. He looked just like a plush toy come to life.

"Here, you clumsy cub. Slowly," she encouraged Max. She eased him next to the bowl again, dipped her finger in the milk and put it near Max's mouth. He licked hungrily, following Stella's finger as she drew him towards the milk bowl. As soon as he found the milk, Max lapped eagerly. Stella had to pull him back gently to stop him from putting his paws in the bowl and knocking it over.

The more Stella watched Max, the more her heart warmed to him. I can do it, she thought. I can surely look after Max and save him from whatever danger he has got himself in. There was only one problem, Stella thought. How could she keep Max hidden from her parents? She somehow had the idea that they would not approve of her keeping Max. She had to come up with an idea. She needed to disguise him in some way or hide him...

"Of course!" she exclaimed, recalling how difficult it had been to spot Max nestled between her soft toys on the bed. "I'll hide him between Mummintroll and Peo Teddy. I'll slip all three in the soft bag I use for when I go to a sleepover at Emilie's house."

Stella frowned, picked Max up and rubbed her nose on his. "I'll have to disguise you a bit, dress you up, like Mummintroll in his striped overalls." She cradled him in her arms again and smiled at the thought of Max in a bonnet and overalls.

Stella was so pleased she had found a solution. Now, she could take Max around with her without anyone making a fuss and asking silly questions.

"Come to think of it, Max and Mumintroll are just as white and their ears are very similar," mused Stella. "I know the plan will be just perfect!"

Chapter Glossary

Klappa - Black or white popular Swedish plush toy

Mumintroll- Favorite cartoon character with Swedish kids.

Chapter Questions

1. What food did Stella give max for breakfast?
2. Who woke up first in the morning?

CHAPTER FOUR

THE TRUTH ABOUT MAX

After feeding Max, Stella rummaged about in her wardrobe looking for something to dress him in. She found an old pale blue jumper of hers and a woolen hat of the Stockholm ice hockey team. Her father had bought it at the Arena Globe, where Stella had watched in awe, as the huge padded ice-hockey players whizzed around on the ice under the immense globe flooded with multi-colored lights.

"Perfect," she exclaimed, "all I have to do is cut the sleeves, here and here." She paused and turned around to look at Sofi, who was following Stella's movements, ears pricked up and tail wagging.

"Do you think I should put some socks on those paws? His claws are really sharp."

Sofi's tail stopped thumping the floor, and her eyebrows rose.

"Hmm maybe not," added Stella," he would look silly with socks."

Stella went back to the bed to cuddle Max again, but he was fast asleep. "I'll slip out now he's sleeping," said Stella to Sofi," if I don't make an appearance downstairs, someone will soon come looking for me."

It was Saturday, and on Saturdays Stella usually slept a bit longer. But she was in no mood for sleeping, and she was getting hungry. So was Sofi, who was trying to dig her nose in Stella's pockets.

"Are you looking for your biscuits?" said Stella remembering the biscuits she had hidden there for Max.

She gave one to Sofi and tugged gently at her pet's long silky ears. Stella then hid the rest of the biscuits in her scrap box, which she kept on her desk. She had forgotten all about trying to feed Max with her pet's biscuits.

"I might have to soften them up a bit with milk," she mused, looking over at Max who was well hidden amongst her soft toys.

She could just make out his soft furry tummy rising and falling gently. She knelt beside the bed and watched him. He sighed and is mouth fell open, the tip of his pink tongue poked out.

"You are the most adorable little animal I've ever seen," she whispered in adoration.

Stella's grumbled suddenly. Now she was very hungry. Max was sound asleep so she could safely leave him.

"Time for breakfast," she said, carefully pushing herself up from the bed so as not to wake Max.

Sofi eagerly followed her mistress downstairs into the kitchen, where Stella's grandpa was sitting at the table with a cup of black coffee and his morning newspaper.

"Hej, god morgon," said Gustav peeping over his newspaper with a beaming smile.

Stella went over to her grandpa and gave him a hug. "God morgon Farfar, is mamma still in bed?"

Gustav nodded, his smile fading a little. "She needs

all the rest she can get today. This evening will be a big event for her too. She's so proud and excited for you, and that tires her out a lot."

Stella's eyes dropped and she looked away. She busied herself getting Sofi's breakfast. She wanted to push away the sad thoughts that were flooding her head.

Sometimes, Stella wished she could turn back the magic watch to when her mother was well and happy. Full of energy and joy. Stella just hoped one day, very soon, mamma would get better. They would then go ice skating in the Kungsträdgården park as they used to a few years before. Her mother was an excellent ice skater, not like her father who could not stand up straight on the ice.

Gustav watched his grand-daughter, his eyes a little more watery than usual. He thought he would cheer Stella up with a funny story he had been reading in the newspaper.

"Listen to this Stella," he said, calling her by her name, although he preferred calling her 'Stjärna'. But Stella did not like nicknames, she thought they were for babies.

"Polar Bear Cub disappears at Skansen. Zoo staff suspect kidnapping. Max the 2-month-year-old cub went missing last night after the staff fed him before his bedtime..."

Stella's eyes opened wide, and she nearly dropped Sofi's bowl. She could not believe her ears. She wasn't sure if she was more surprised by the news, or by the fact that Max's name was indeed Max. Stella took this as a decisive sign. She was destined to take care of him, and she was even more convinced after she heard what her grandpa was about to add.

"Baby Max is the surviving cub of three, his brother and sister were not as lucky. Their mum, Licka fell ill after giving birth to her cubs. The zoo staff have been hand feeding Max since then, and he was doing fine until last night when he mysteriously disappeared..."

Max's mother could not take care of him! But Stella could, and she would. She would save him and love him just like his mum would have done.

Stella tried to appear as normal as possible. She was afraid to reveal too much to her grandpa. Although he was her best friend she was not sure he would agree to keep Max. Her grandpa was very crafty, sometimes Stella wondered if he could read her thoughts.

"Oh, poor little bear," she exclaimed trying to

look surprised, while her thoughts went to her adorable friend sleeping soundly on her bed, "I hope they find him soon."

"Yes indeed, I hope they do. I fear they've kidnapped him to sell him to some crazy rich man who has decided to open his own private zoo," said Gustav frowning angrily at the thought. "Wild animals should be left in the wild. They are not toys to cuddle and play with."

Stella's face flushed red and she went over to the fridge to keep away from her grandpa's gaze. She was sure he was reading her thoughts now. But he was a real nature lover and he was probably just reacting to the news.

She knew from his incredible stories, that when he was young he had worked for the forestry department up in the north of Sweden. He had spent all his working years in close contact with nature. That was when he had encountered Leo, amongst other wild animals.

Stella nearly told her grandpa there and then, not to worry about Max. She did not like seeing her grandpa upset. But she was still not sure she could trust him.

Stella finished her yoghurt and cereal as fast as she could without arousing suspicion, then decided it was time to get on with her plan.

She spent the morning in her room, only briefly going in to kiss her mother, who stayed in bed most of the day. But to Stella's relief mamma looked better than usual, her face was not as pale and her eyes even twinkled.

At one point Stella sneaked Max downstairs with Sofi. He needed some fresh air and a pee and poop. He had already peed on her bed... She eased him in the green and blue soft bag she used for overnight stays and was relieved to see he fitted just fine.

"I'll stuff Mummintroll and maybe Pippi or Alfie too. Max will be in good company and best of all, well hidden," Stella pondered out loud.

Sofi trotted after Stella into the garden behind the shed. Stella let Max out and kept a close eye on him. He was still clumsy and fell over a lot, but he could stumble along quite a way in the snow. Here, his claws gripped more securely to the ground. He even managed to venture around the shed, his nose twitching as he smelt his way in the garden. Stella who had been distracted by Sofi, rushed to pick him up and plonked him back behind the shed out of view.

After lunch, when Max was sleeping again. Stella

went downstairs with Sofi to practice her violin in the sitting room for her grandpa.

"You play wondrously," exclaimed Gustav," much, much better than your pappa and I ever did. You'll be the star of the show tonight."

Stella beamed at her grandfather. "Will you sit in the front row so I can see you Farfar?"

"Oh, you won't even notice there is an audience in the theatre," exclaimed Gustav, "you'll be swept away by the lights, music and magic of the place. But of course, I will. I will insist on sitting on the front row right in front the best violinist in the orchestra."

Stella got up and put her violin away with great care, then went over to her grandpa and gave him a hug. "I'd better start getting ready," she said, her eyes shining with excitement.

"Just one thing Stella before you go... Something's been tickling at my curiosity all day. Can you tell me if that was Sofi I saw out in the garden this morning? If it was she must have changed color." Gustav's eyes were twinkling with humor as he looked into Stella's.

Stella swallowed hard. Her stomach tightened. She did not like telling lies, but she was scared that grandpa would be cross with her and take Max away.

"Well, huh, you know how Sofi loves rolling in the snow Farfar," Stella replied, her voice shaking a little.

"She certainly does," agreed Gustav his smile wider now.

Stella's eyes widened with anxiety. She stared at her grandpa searching his eyes to see if she could trust him. Her shoulders dropped and her head bent over.

"Please Farfar, don't tell pappa and mamma."

Her grandpa shook his head. "Of course, I won't." He took her in his arms and gave her a huge hug.

Stella let out a sigh of relief. She breathed in her grandpa's familiar smell of tobacco, which was strangely comforting. He was still her best friend.

"I don't know how you found him. But if you did it was no doubt to save him from a bad fate," Gustav added.

Stella nodded vigorously, relieved by his words. Her grandpa always knew what was right.

"You won't ask me to take Max back to the zoo, will you?" Stella said her voice full of anxiety.

"The zoo? Of course, not. Max doesn't belong to a zoo he belongs to nature." He scrunched his white eyebrows. "We'll have to think out a good plan. But for the time being, we should make sure he gets all he needs. Food and lots of love."

Stella's spirits rose again. She knew she could count on her grandpa to help her with Max. He knew so many things about wild animals. He was the wisest person in the world.

"Now, will you introduce me to Max please," asked Gustav with a wink.

Chapter Glossary

The Globe Arena - the largest spherical building in the world with an inside-height of up to 85 meters. It is the symbol for the city of Stockholm and Sweden. With a seating capacity of 13.850 for hockey.

Hej, god morgon - Hello Good morning

Kungsträdgården -Kungsträdgården's open-air ice-skating rink in Stockholm with stands selling hot drinks.

Stjärna- star

Chapter Questions

1. What did Stella dress max in?
2. What was Stella's nickname her grandfather called her?
3. What did Stella use to hide max in downstairs?

CHAPTER FIVE

FARFAR AND STELLA COME UP WITH A PLAN

"Is everyone ready," shouted Alexander from the bottom of the stairs.

Stella was bursting with excitement for two reasons. One, she was fretting to step through the doors of the magnificent opera house, and two, her grandpa had agreed to bring Max along.

She closed her eyes briefly and imagined herself walking through the plush decor into the theatre. The spotlights would flood the stage, and the murmur of the audience would hush before the beginning of the concert.

Her grandpa had reasoned that they could not leave Max alone, or he would probably get into trouble. He had loved the idea of carrying him in a bag and it seemed to work perfectly. They had also dressed Max up to disguise him among the other toys.

"He looks so funny, Farfar. Especially with the ice-hockey hat on his head. It hides his ears well though. He twitches them quite a lot, even when he sleeps," said Stella, as they rehearsed their plan once more before leaving. "Won't mamma disagree on me bringing along a bag as well as my violin?"

"Don't you worry about that. I'll take care of your mother's questions, and of the bag too. You just get on and play as beautifully as you always do," said Gustav easing Max into the soft bag.

Stella was less nervous then she thought she would be. She was so excited about Max and his first evening out, that she forgot all about being jittery. She even forgot about Sofi, whose floppy ears dropped back and brown eyes sulked as she eyed Stella getting ready. Sofi was not allowed to go to the restaurant and concert. She would be left all alone in the house.

"Coming," shouted Stella back as she tried to do up the bow on the back of her black and white velvet dress. It was a beautiful dress her mother had bought in the shops especially for this occasion, but the ribbon was impossible to tie up.

"You go on downstairs and get pappa to do up the ribbon. I'll follow with Max, Mummintroll and Peo," said Gustav, who was hopeless at ribbons and such things.

Stella skipped downstairs, peeping into the soft bag before leaving the bedroom. Max was curled up against Mummintroll, the woolen hat slightly skewed, and only one eye visible.

Gustav came downstairs at the last minute. Alexander was getting impatient and was in too much of a hurry to notice the soft bag Gustav was carrying over his shoulder. He shooed them outside where the family Volvo was waiting, engine running.

Emma was already in the passenger seat. She smiled at Stella from the window. Stella's eyes met her mother's in the rear-view mirror when she sat in the back with her grandfather. Her mother's eyes glowed with happiness and warmed Stella's heart.

Gustav settled in next to Stella placing the soft bag between them. "I brought a few of my favorite toys," said Stella, her blue eyes wide and innocent as she looked at her mother.

"If it helps you feel less nervous, that's fine my dear," answered Emma. She was feeling stronger and happier on this special night and in no mood to get fussy or cross.

They drove through the cold February evening, the city lights shimmering, like fairies suspended in the icy air. They passed the old city of Gamla and crossed the Strömbron bridge. Stella rubbed her gloved hand over the fogged-up window and pressed her face on the cold glass. She marveled at the sparkling colors reflected in the still waters of the River Norrström. Stockholm by night reminded Stella of a fantasy land.

The car came to a sudden stop, waking Stella from her reverie. She recognized the magnificent Kungliga Operan and wondered why they had come here so early. She had thought they were all going for a special meal before the concert.

Stella felt a bit let down, but she pretended everything was fine. She did not want to ruin everyone's good mood, by being fussy.

She had never been to the opera at night before. The magnificent front was flooded with lights projected up from the ground. They reminded Stella of geysers of brilliant water gushing up onto the walls. A group of people were standing outside, dressed in elegant clothes and glittering jewels. Stella felt so tiny and awestruck and doubted whether she would be able to step out of the car.

"Quick, everybody out while I go and park the car," said Alexander as he pulled up to the curb.

They all piled out and stood there on the pavement as if under a spell. Grandpa was clutching the bag with Max, and Emma had her arms wrapped around Stella, who was staring opened mouthed at the enormous entrance. Alexander soon came trotting around the corner of the imposing building towards them.

"So, what are we waiting for? Let's go in!" exclaimed Alexander taking Emma and Stella by the arm.

They climbed up the short flight of stone steps and pushed through the wood and glass doors into the small elegant entrance hall.

Stella breathed in the delicious aromas floating about in the confined recess area. She wondered where they were coming from. She was even more puzzled when they turned left, instead of taking the stairs up to the main theatre hall, but she followed without questioning.

"And here, is the famous Operan Brasserie one of the most prestigious restaurants in Stockholm," announced Alexander with a bow and a sweep of his arm.

Stella's mouth dropped. She was staring at the entrance of what looked like a stage set for one of those historical films her mother sometimes watched on television.

"What is a restaurant doing in the opera house," asked Stella her eyes wide with amazement.

Alexander chuckled in amusement, "it's been specially opened for hungry little girls who play in concerts."

Stella blinked twice and pulled a face at her father. Then beamed and gave him a big hug.

"This is the most fantastic surprise ever pappa," said Stella, now guessing that this was the surprise her mother had been hinting at.

They stepped into the vast dining room with its large columns painted gold and light blue. There were even intimate alcoves for private dining, with white arched walls and ornate golden pictures. The light was soft and diffused over the tables draped with crisp white linen. There were no chairs, but plush leather couches that reminded Stella of milk chocolate bars. Golden side plates and cutlery were neatly set on the tables, and in their center, candles glowed in frosted glass holders.

Every single object shone. "This is what Aladdin felt like when he entered the famous treasure cave," said Stella under her breath.

And indeed, the dinner was the most special one Stella had ever had. There were so many different dishes to savor, of all assorted colors and tastes. The plates were swept away elegantly, and new, clean ones were placed in front of them.

During dinner, Stella noticed that grandpa's hand disappeared under the table quite a few times. At one point, when her mother and father were talking and smiling to one another, Stella leant over to her grandpa and whispered, "can Max actually eat things?"

"Of course, he can," whispered back Gustav, "and he loves the trout in butter sauce."

Stella glanced over at her parents, as she slipped a teaspoon of vanilla ice cream under the table to Max. She nearly squealed out loud when she felt Max's tongue eagerly lick the spoon and her hand. Her mother was smiling radiantly, just as she used to before she got sick. Alexander had an arm around her shoulder, his eyes alight with joy.

Suddenly, the tablecloth started slipping from under Stella's hand, and she panicked when she realized it was Max tugging the material. Two plates nearly slid off onto the plush maroon carpet with swirly white motifs.

'Oh," exclaimed Gustav, "who's a clumsy old man tonight." He caught the plates just in time, and carefully placed them on the table. He then turned to smile at Stella, who had turned ghastly pale. Fortunately, no one had noticed under the restaurant's diffused lights.

Stella could not imagine what she would have done without her grandpa. He always knew how to get out of any trouble.

When the meal was over they followed Alexander into the main hall. He carried Stella's violin and walked with Emma ahead of Stella and her grandpa. Gustav was still holding the soft bag, from which the tip of the ice-hockey hat and one of Mummintroll's ears were visible. Stella could not wait to cuddle Max again and rub her nose into his soft fur. But when she entered the enormous inner hall and stood at the foot of the wide marble staircase with its golden railings, Stella forgot all about Max.

Her stomach churned and her heart beat faster. She was in the Kungliga Operan. This was her big night; a night she would never forget. She was floating in this dreamlike atmosphere, through threads of music that drifted from the open dark Oakwood doors. The musty odor of the wooden paneling and pungent aroma of the waxed floors tickled at her nostrils. Stella was in a dream land.

Stella played that night, she played as she had never played before. Her bow danced on the strings of her violin like magic fingers. When Stella finally reached the end, she heard thunder. A deafening clapping filled her ears and tears flooded her eyes. She had done it. She had played right through a concert at the famous Stockholm opera house, and the audience was cheering.

When Stella exited through the backstage she was submerged by a flurry of emotions. Both her parents were there to greet her. The both took her in their arms. Grandpa came to hug her and planted a loud kiss on her forehead. Everyone talked at once making Stella's head spin.

"You played like a star, Stella," said her mother

beaming, but now visibly tired from the evening events. Alexander took Emma's arm and added, "The best Stella, we are so proud, you are a hundred times better than Farfar, and maybe even better than me."

Stella's grandpa frowned at his son and scolded him. "That may be true son, but you should never have given up the violin. You're lucky Stella will make up for your neglect."

"Enough of your wise words Pop." Alexander glanced over at Emma and added, "it's time to go home now, we're all tired even if happy. But before the evening ends, I still have a surprise to announce."

Stella's mouth dropped open. Another surprise. She thought the opera restaurant had been the surprise. Her grandpa was also taken aback, which was rare for him, he even dropped the soft bag with Max in it. Stella crossed her fingers and toes that Max would not tumble out.

"As you played so magnificently Stella, I have treated you all to the Ice Hotel. We are leaving for the Lapland on the Arctic Circle Night train next Friday for the weekend." Alexander stood there beaming while Stella and grandpa just gaped at him, lost for words.

"Wh... where?" cried out Stella waking up from her

shock.

"THE Ice Hotel, where guests sleep in rooms sculpted in ice and ride on sledges pulled by reindeer. At this time of the year, we'll be able to admire the spectacle of the Northern lights." Alexander replied.

Without a word, Stella leapt into her father's arms and covered him with kisses. The Ice Hotel was the most amazing place Stella had ever heard of, and they were taking the night train! She had to stop herself from jumping up and down with excitement, thinking of how happy Max would be. He would adore it in the Lapland, he would feel at home in the snow and ice.

When Stella took her grandpa's hand as they left the opera house, she beamed at him and noticed he was still wide-eyed, staring ahead deep in thought.

"What's the matter Farfar? Is something wrong?"

"Wrong? No of course not, everything is absolutely perfect," Gustav exclaimed. He had picked up his pace and his eyes were shining. He was also squeezing Stella's hand a bit too hard. He slowed down a little letting Stella's parents go ahead so they would be out of ear's reach. Then he turned to face Stella, his eyes ablaze with excitement.

"Max, Stella. We can take Max to Leo. Set him free

into the wilderness, where he belongs," he said with intensity.

Stella's stomach tightened. Max needed her. She was not as sure as her grandfather that this was a promising idea. But she decided to dismiss the thought, and pulled at her grandfather's hand, a frown still on her brow. She would find a way to reason with him once they were in Jukkasjarvi.

Chapter glossary

Strömbron (The Stream Bridge) - 140 meters long bridge in central Stockholm. It crosses over the Norrström River connecting the old city Gamla to the central mainland.

Jukkasjarvi - The town where the Ice hotel is situated - Lapland Sweden.

Chapter questions

1. What was Gustav’s idea for hiding Max?
2. What did Stella wear for her violin concert?
3. What did Stockholm’s nightly views remind Stella of?
4. What was the name of the restaurant inside the opera house?
5. What did Stella give max to eat under the dinner table?

C H A P T E R S I X

THE ARTIC CIRCLE TRAIN

"Do you have to take the bag with all those stuffed toys?" asked Emma when she saw Stella coming down the stairs lugging the soft bag along.

"Come on Emma, it's a long way away from home, and a kid needs her comfort favorite's," slipped in Gustav, who was following behind Stella.

Stella sighed with relief. Her grandpa had saved the day yet again. However, he was right, it was a long trip to the little Sami town of Juskkasjarvi. It would take them about sixteen hours to get to the Lapland. Stella thought how exciting it would be to travel through the night and snow, speeding across the northern winter landscape.

She and her grandpa were sharing a sleeper car. She had never slept on a train before and was bursting with anticipation. She was just a little anxious about Max. It would not be easy to smuggle him on the train. What if they looked into the bag? Butterflies swirled around her stomach. she was at once excited by the journey, but also anxious about keeping Max hidden.

It was late afternoon when they left their house on Skogvaktargatan in the Hjorthagen district. They lived close to the 'Deer Park' opposite the Vartan Strait at only a fifteen minute' drive to the central station.

The train station was close to the opera house, where she had played barely a week before. It all seemed far off now. The lights, the music and the thrill of the atmosphere a vague memory.

Tonight, they were embarking on the most fantastic adventure ever. The Swedish Lapland was so far north it seemed almost unreachable. Stella knew that many people loved visiting the area for its natural beauty, but that only a few had actually slept in the Ice Hotel. She would go skiing and sledging with Max, and even ride on sledges drawn by real reindeer. They would have so much fun together with Max and Farfar.

Stella's father dropped them off with their bags in front of the imposing station and went to park the car. The station was bustling with travelers, and the evening air was filled with the misty night chill and bright station lights. Stella's head was swirling as she fidgeted on the spot to keep warm. She could not wait to board the Arctic circle train.

They finally entered the enormous glass dome station's hall with its shiny marble floor. There were shops and cafés with people sitting at tables, while others rushed to catch their trains. Stepping into the grand central station was like walking into another dimension. It was like a city in a city. A thrill of excitement rushed through Stella's body as they stood under the big timetable board to search for their platform number. They were in the north terminal from where all the trains heading north left.

Platform 7, leaving in fifteen minutes," announced

Alexander, urging them to move along with a sweep of his hand. Gustav and Stella held hands as they followed Alexander and Emma through to the vast hall towards the platform area.

"How's Max doing?" whispered Stella to her grandpa as they hurried along.

"Fast asleep as usual," replied Gustav giving her a reassuring smile.

They were about to go through into the platform area when they were stalled by a security barrier checkpoint just before the platforms.

"This is unusual," muttered Alexander under his breath. He was visibly irritated by the unexpected delay and there were quite a few people queueing up. They had to wait behind a middle-aged couple who were arguing with the man at the checkpoint wearing a blue and red uniform and a cap.

Stella's heart skipped. What would happen if the man in the uniform checked their bags and found Max? Then she would really be in trouble. The lady in front of them kept rummaging in her large black leather bag. Alexander started getting impatient. He kept checking his watch and glancing above the passengers' heads towards the platforms.

Stella was also getting nervous. She hoped they would not miss the train. That would be a disaster. What was that woman fussing for anyway? Now Emma started getting restless and threw nervous glances at Alexander and back at Stella's grandpa.

"Are we going to be late," whispered Stella to her grandpa. She did not want to appear anxious or be a nuisance, but she was getting worried now.

"Hem mm," Alexander cleared his throat to attract the controller's attention and held out a hand with the four tickets waving them in the air.

"I'm sorry to interrupt, but our train is leaving in 10 minutes from platform 7."

The controller lifted his eyes from the ticket he was holding and eyed Stella's father suspiciously. "You should arrive earlier, this is a large station and platform 7 is right at the far end."

Emma came to the rescue. She noticed that her husband was getting more and more irritated, especially after the controllers' rude remark. "Oh dear, you are perfectly right. We are sorry, it was all my fault," she excused herself with a radiant smile, "I was silly enough to forget my handbag at home, and my husband had to drive back to fetch it."

The controller eyed Emma too, but his expression softened. He then waved his hand impatiently, signaling for them to go through. He did not even give their tickets one glance. Alexander took Emma by the hand and broke into a fast trot with Stella and Gustav trailing behind, the bag with Max bouncing up and down.

Stella was out of breath when they finally reached their platform. The engines were humming and the train was ready to leave. Stella was shaking with relief. They had just reached the train on time and had escaped the encounter with the man in uniform.

"That was close," panted Gustav, who although was in good shape for his age, needed some time to recover from the rush to the platform. Alexander climbed onto the train first to carry the bags on board, he then helped Emma get on. While Stella waited on the platform with her panting grandpa, she noticed two large curvy initials on the side of the carriage.

"S. J," Stella read out loud, "Stella Johansson, this must be my train." Stella beamed at her grandpa. "It feels great to travel on a train with my initials," she said proudly.

Although grandpa insisted that this did not mean the train was hers, Stella paid no attention. She wanted to pretend this was her private train for the night.

Stella climbed in after her mother and Alexander helped her grandpa on.

"Pass me that soft bag Gustav," said Alexander noticing that the bag was getting in his way. Stella's grandpa had no choice, he passed the bag over to Alexander who dropped it on the floor with a thud.

To her horror, Stella, who was just behind her father, saw Max roll out and lose his ice hockey hat. He let out a funny noise she had not heard before.

"Hmm, Hmm," coughed Gustav as Alexander pulled him up into the train, trying to cover Max's squawk because that was exactly how it sounded.

Alexander patted Gustav on his back gently. "Are you alright pappa?" he asked with a frown, worried that Stella's grandpa had had more than his share, with the rush through the station. Meanwhile, Stella took advantage of the commotion and pushed Max back into the bag and pulled the hat back over his ears. Stella was getting anxious again. They would have to find their sleeping car fast before Max made another of his strange noises.

"Carriage 4, sleeping cabins 26 and 28," announced Alexander as he took the lead down the narrow corridor. Stella followed right behind her grandfather, using him as a cover. She was now holding the bag in her arms, one hand deep in Max's fur, stroking him to soothe the little bear.

They finally found their sleeping cabins, which were one next to the other.

"You two settle down," said Alexander to Stella and Gustav, "while I get mamma comfortable. That was a bit too much excitement for her and you too pappa."

As she entered the elegant and cozy cabin, Stella thought that she too had had a bit too much excitement. It was neatly furnished with two beds, one on top of the other. Bunk beds were Stella's favorite’s. She put down the bag on the bottom bed and sighed loudly. She then took off her shoes and jumped up onto the top bed. She bounced up and down until she bumped her head on the low ceiling and lay down giggling.

Stella's grandpa closed the door to their sleeping cabin and sat down heavily, letting out a big sigh. Stella hung her head down over the top bed and watched him as he reached into the inner pocket of his coat and opened a round tin box. He fished out one of his mini teabags, the 'snus' tobacco he liked so much and slipped one under his upper lip.

"Farfar, you should stop that bad habit," scolded Stella.

Gustav raised his eyebrows and his hands in surrender. "More than half the men in Sweden use it, and anyway, I needed that. What with all the fuss we've been through since we arrived at the station."

Stella thought it was a funny habit. Most grandpas smoked pipes or cigars. At least the tiny teabags did not stink. They were supposed to be less harmful than real smoke, although she doubted that was true. Stella forgot all about the 'snus' when Max poked his head out of the bag and made that funny noise again.

"It's the first time I've heard him make that noise. It sounds more like a crow than a bear," Stella exclaimed puzzled.

"Yes, it's funny isn't it," replied Gustav, now looking visibly more relaxed. "They do that when they get impatient and restless. I think he's trying to tell us he's hungry."

Stella jumped down again and opened the bag she had packed for the weekend. She pulled out a special mix her grandpa had shown her how to make for Max. He loved it.

Stella watched her white furry friend as he lapped the thick milk mix. She suddenly thought of Sofi and felt guilty about leaving her behind. She had asked her father if they could bring Sofi along, but she had not really insisted when he had said no.

"Really, Stella, we can't have an animal with us on the train. We'll be too busy to pay attention to Sofi. Besides, the Ice hotel does not allow pets."

A low piercing screech sounded from outside. Stella went to the window and pushed it ajar to take a peep outside. Her nostrils filled with the cold evening air, and she heard the doors of the carriages banging shut. One more whistle and the train jolted and jerked forward, then slowly moved out of the station. The adventure on the Arctic Circle Night train had begun.

Chapter Questions

1. How long was the train ride?
2. What was Stella looking forward to at the ice hotel?
3. What did Stella notice about the train carriage?
4. What did Gustav do when they reached their sleeping beds?
5. What did Stella feed max?

CHAPTER SEVEN

THE NIGHT ADVENTURE

The train pulled out of the station with a groan. It gradually picked up speed as it left the platform behind and headed north towards Jukkasjarvi and the Ice hotel.

Stella pressed her face against the window. She watched the city lights whizz by, her eyes quivering back and forth to keep up with the fleeting sights.

It was dark outside by now, and once they had left

the city glare behind Stella could hardly make out the landscape. Now and then she spotted patches of snow, but somber woodland and darkness were all she could see now.

Stella decided it was time to explore the train. She was looking forward to dinner in the restaurant carriage and wanted to find out where it was. Stella was also getting tired and thought of what fun it would be to snuggle up into her small cot while hurtling through the winter night. But she was too excited to think of sleep for the moment.

"Can I go and explore the train Farfar?" asked Stella tearing herself from the window.

"Yes of course. But don't get into mischief and don't be away too long," Gustav replied. His upper lip bulging comically because of the 'snus'.

Max had fallen asleep again on her grandpa's bunk-bed. His ears twitching back and forward even as he slept.

"Polar bear cubs do sleep a lot," frowned Stella. "I can't even show Max around the train."

"You certainly can't, "rebuked Gustav, "the railway staff won't look kindly on us if they find out we're carrying a polar bear around. They'll think we're the kidnappers and have us arrested immediately," said Gustav with a frown.

“Oh dear,” said Stella raising her fair eyebrows in alarm, “I hadn’t thought of that.” She scrunched her brow, deep in thought.” What if we tell them that we’re on a secret mission and that the zoo has hired us to take Max to the Lapland.” Stella nodded with satisfaction, thinking it was a sensible excuse.

But her grandpa shook his head. “We’re not going to tell anyone anything of the sort.”

He mused for a few seconds, moving the ‘snus’ around under his upper lip. “I suppose we are, but we must keep Max hidden until we get to the Lapland.”

Stella wondered what her grandpa was referring to. She had only invented the story for fun, but he seemed to take it seriously.

“Alright Farfar, I’ll keep my lips sealed,” she said pursing her lips tightly. “I’ll just snoop around a bit and be back before dinner.”

Stella popped her head into the corridor and looked right and left. Some people were still dragging their luggage along the corridor as they searched their sleeping cabins. She would make her way towards the head of the train first. She was quite sure that was where the restaurant carriage was. Stella wanted to have a quick look at the menu. She was starving already.

Stella stepped out into the long corridor and closed the door behind her. She pressed her ear against the door of her parent's cabin, all was silent. Her mother was probably having a rest after all the excitement at the station. She headed towards the front of the train holding her hands out beside her, as the train gently jostled to and fro.

There were so many sleeping cabins all along the corridor, but there did not seem to be many passengers on the train. The man and woman she had seen in the corridor had now disappeared. They had no doubt found their cabin. Stella reached the end of the carriage and pushed the automatic button to pass through the glass doors into the next carriage.

The train was picking up speed now, and Stella had to hold on. When she stepped into the next carriage she lost her balance and bumped into someone going in the opposite direction.

"Oh!" said a deep voice from above her. Stella looked up into a red-faced man. He had a blue and red uniform and a cap, just like the man checking people at the train station. She mumbled an apology and was about to walk on when the man in uniform stopped her.

"Where are you going little girl?" he said frowning at Stella. "Shouldn't you be with your parents? I'll be coming around to check everyone's tickets soon, so you'd better get back to your cabin."

His bushy eyebrows were bunched up and his long thin nose stuck out from his face like a beak. "You mustn't get in the way of the railway staff, they're busy getting the service ready now."

Stella did not like this big red-faced man, she could tell he was not to be trusted. She disliked adults who tried to scare you out of doing things, instead of talking sensibly. Stella's grandpa always talked nicely to her. He also listened and valued her opinion.

"Hem, I was just looking for the toilet," Stella replied, not finding a better excuse.

"Now that will depend on where your cabin is, young lady. Passengers should always use the toilets closest to their cabins," said the man sternly.

Stella disliked the man more and more, and she thought he was somewhat of a bully too. She did not want to tell him where her cabin was and did not trust him one bit.

Stella was picking up her courage to protest. She

wanted to point out that if someone was walking along the corridor or was in another part of the train, he or she would surely be allowed to pee in someone else's toilet.

But the ticket controller went on. "Now let me follow you back to your parents' cabin and I'll show you which toilets and shower room you can use."

Stella's arms dropped. She could not think of any other excuse to get away from the man, all she could do was obey. So, she turned back towards their cabin.

"My parents are in this cabin and I'm in the next one with my grandfather who is resting now. He's a very old and mustn't be disturbed when he sleeps," said Stella her eyes wide with concern.

"Craaoook," came a strange noise from behind the cabin door. The ticket collector's white bushy eyebrows lifted in surprise.

"What was that?" he boomed, his face getting redder.

Stella's face paled, and she opened her mouth but no words came out. The door suddenly opened and Gustav's face poked out through the gap in the doorway.

"Cough! Cough! Achoo om!" Stella's grandpa bent down and sneezed loudly in his handkerchief again. "Oh, dear I'm sorry," he said, his blue watery eyes filled with tears, as he broke into another bout of coughing. "It must be all this dust on the train."

"Dust?" exclaimed the ticket collector, "the cleaning staff are very efficient on our train line. The train is sparkling clean when it leaves Stockholm station."

Stella's eyes lit up. Her grandpa always had such clever ideas, she thought proudly. She had heard Max's noises from behind the door and her grandpa had come to the rescue. It was now her turn. "You do make such funny noises Farfar, when you have one of your sneezing fits," she giggled.

"Yes, indeed, very strange noises," commented the ticket collector with a frown. "They sounded more like animal noises," he added, craning his neck to look past Gustav and into the cabin.

Stella felt the blood in her head drop to her feet. She crossed her fingers and toes that Max would not make a noise right now.

Fortunately, they were saved by her father, who opened the door to the next cabin.

"What's going on?" he said looking at Stella who was standing just outside his cabin door. Then he noticed the ticket collector and smiled, “Oh, let me get our tickets. I have a total of four, including my daughter’s and fathers who are next to my wife and me, as you can see.”

The ticket collector opened his mouth to complain that this was nothing to do with ticket collecting, but Stella’s father disappeared into the cabin. He was back a few seconds later with their tickets in hand. He grinned at the ticket collector. “Here they are. We’re going right to Jukkasjarvi to the Ice hotel,” he said enthusiastically as he handed them over to him.

The ticket collector took the tickets and simply nodded, not at all impressed with their destination.

“Yes sir, all in order,” he growled,” I was telling your daughter that if you need the toilet and shower facilities you are to use those ones over there.” He nodded towards the back of the carriage. “Wc prefer passengers use their section of the train,” he added curtly.

“Of course, I’ll make sure my family does just that,” said Alexander smiling politely at the ticket collector.

Not having any more reason to complain, the ticket collector nodded at Stella’s father. He eyed Stella and Gustav suspiciously before heading back the way they had come.

"That's settled then," said Alexander with a smile at Stella and Gustav. "What was all that sneezing and coughing papa," he asked frowning, "I hope you're not going to get ill for the weekend."

"No, no, nonsense," replied Gustav with a shake of his head, "I'm fine."

"Good," said Alexander, "you two get ready for supper, we'll be going in less than twenty minutes. Emma just needed a little rest before dinner." He then slipped back into the cabin and closed the door.

Stella turned to her grandpa and her shoulders dropped as she let out a big sigh. "That was real, close," she whispered.

Her grandpa looked down along the corridor, his eyebrows scrunched and his mouth puckered slightly as if deep in thought.

"We had better keep a close eye on that man. I have a feeling he can't be trusted. We don't need trouble before we get to the ice hotel."

Stella shuddered, she was looking forward to the weekend on the snow with Max, she did not want that terrible man to ruin their fun. Her grandpa was right. They had to be on the watch out.

Chapter questions

1. Where did max fall asleep?
2. Who did Stella say she disliked?
3. What did Gustav say was the source of the strange coughing?

CHAPTER EIGHT

WHERE IS MAX

To Stella's relief, they finally managed to get to the restaurant car. She thought she would never get there for some odd reason. She kept thinking of the ticket collector and his odd behavior.

"He wasn't very nice, was he?" said Stella to her grandpa, who was sitting next to her in the restaurant booth.

"No, he wasn't," said Gustav, knowing who Stella was talking about without having to ask. Stella and her grandpa spent a lot of time together when she was not at school or with her friend Emilie. Stella's grandpa always seems to know what she was thinking about.

"What a silly thing to say," she went on her eyes flashing, "I mean, why shouldn't we be allowed to use the toilets?"

Emma who was sitting just across from Stella looked up and frowned. "Who told you can't use the toilets? Of course, you can Stella my dear."

Stella's grandpa shook his head and smiled. "Stella, he didn't say you couldn't use the toilets. He told us to use the ones closest to our sleeping berths."

Stella frowned and rested her chin in her hand, both elbows on the table. "Well, what if I want to go to the toilet now? Do I have to go right back along the corridor to our berth?"

"Don't be silly Stella, there are toilets right next to the restaurant car," replied Alexander who was getting exasperated with the conversation.

"Right," said Stella taking her elbows off the table and picking up the elegant menu, "That was exactly my point. The man was just being nasty."

Stella's grandpa lifted both hands, palms up. "Don't be too rough on him Stella, he's probably not happy about having to work all night."

Stella commented with a 'humph', then continued to study the menu, her eyes lighting up at the choice of delicious dishes.

The restaurant car was nice and cozy. On each table were tiny shimmering lights that looked like candles and real tablecloths. The booths were lined up next to the windows on either side of the corridor. Stella was sitting right next to the window and could look outside as they ate their meal. Not that there was much to see. It was pitch black outside. From time to time, she spotted the lights of a house nestled in the snow-clad countryside and the darker patches of thick fir forests.

Although Stella was enjoying her 'raggmunks', she was a little worried about Max. When they had left for dinner he had been fast asleep on her grandpa's bed. She shook her bad thoughts away thinking that he was safe where he was, and they would not be too long.

The waiter came to collect their plates and asked them if they wanted dessert. Stella forgot all about Max and ordered a princesstårta, which was her favorite. No soon had the princess cake arrived that Stella tucked in it with her spoon.

"Yum," she said, delighting in the delicate taste of the bright green and pink marzipan cake. "I can't think of anything yummier than a princesstårta."

Stella's teaspoon suddenly stopped midway between the plate and her mouth. Her gaze had frozen and she was now looking past her plate and down the aisle. A man had just stepped through the glass doors and was coming towards them. It was the ticket collector.

Stella's eyes darted back to her plate. She scolded herself for getting all flustered about him. But, she could not help it. Sometimes she had bad feelings about people, and this was one of those.

Stella glanced up again just as he passed their table. Had she caught him frown at her? She shook her head and scooped up the last bits of fruit and cream from the plate then looked over the table at her mother.

"Mamma, may I leave the table, please. I'm feeling a bit tired."

"You? Tired?" exclaimed Emma, "I can never get you to bed usually." Emma smiled at Stella and her eyes turned to Gustav. "Farfar, would you mind going with Stella? I don't want her to go wandering off in the train and getting lost."

Stella scrunched her mouth up and frowned. "I will not get lost. It's easy to get around trains all you have to do is follow the corridor. I'm sure no one has ever got lost on a train."

Despite Stella's protests, she was happy to have her grandpa with her. It was no fun exploring places alone and grandpa was not like all the other adults. He was full of fun and mischief, and he always had a clever idea ready for every one of their adventures.

Stella and Gustav left the table and walked along the long corridor towards their sleeping berth.

"Farfar, can we go and fetch Max and take him for a tour of the train?" Stella asked eagerly. She was dying to explore the train with Max and her grandpa.

"Well, we'll see," replied Gustav, "he might still be asleep and you should get some sleep too."

Stella frowned. Her grandpa was usually happy to do daring things, and he was never the one to suggest bedtime. She wondered if he was worried about the ticket collector too.

When they reached the berth, Gustav pulled out the special card that unlocked the door. He pushed the door open and Stella's eyes searched the bottom bed for Max.

Max was not there. She scanned the small compartment, but still no Max. Stella then got down on her knees and lifted the plush duvet that covered the bed and peeped under. There was her bag and her grandpa's bag, but still no Max.

"Where is that naughty cub hiding?" asked Gustav from the washbasin where he was washing his hands. As he dried them on the clean hand towel that they had found on a rack under the washbasin, he looked around frowning.

"He must be in here. I locked the door before we left," he said, his voice now troubled.

He stretched his neck to look on the top bed and pulled the duvet away to get a better look. Max could not have possibly climbed up on the top bed, but he checked just in case.

Stella's voice trembled as she asked, "Farfar where can he be? He's not in here we would have found him by now, it's so small."

Gustav shook his head, his brows now scrunched deep in thought. "I can't imagine how he could have gotten out by himself, unless..." He stopped and faced Stella. "Someone must have opened the door. Someone was snooping in our berth."

Stella's eyes opened wide. Her heart started beating fast. She gasped. "Farfar! Do you think it was that awful ticket collector?"

Gustav's watery blue eyes met Stella's bright blue ones. They were motionless staring at her, deep in thought. At last, he shook his head. "No. It couldn't be. There would have been an upheaval if one of the railway staff had discovered Max. Something else happened. But what can that be?" He mused looking around the berth again.

"There can only be two possible scenarios,' he said finally, after having thought for a few minutes. "One, someone entered by mistake and didn't close the door properly so Max got out. Two, someone came in and took Max, but this someone was not the ticket collector."

"So, who was it?" asked Stella, getting more and more anxious.

"I have no idea Stella. But we should get out there and start looking for him. If he did get away by himself, we might be lucky and find him before someone else does. Most of the passengers are still in the restaurant car or in the lounge area in the front."

Stella pulled at her grandpa's sleeve. "Come on Farfar, let's go and find Max fast before someone else does."

Stella and her grandpa slipped out of their sleeper again. They stood out in the corridor for a few seconds to think. It was still deserted.

"Where could he have gone to?" puzzled Stella.

"Let's go the opposite way we came," said Gustav, "we didn't see him on the way down so he must have headed the other way."

So, off they trotted down the train in thc opposite direction of the restaurant car. They had to hold on now and then, as the train jostled and bumped them from side to side.

A few of the sleeping berths were open and unoccupied. Stella looked in scanning the small berths to check if Max had decided to find another sleeping place. But Max was nowhere to be found.

When they reached the end of the train where the luggage compartment was there was still no sign of the cub.

"He must be here Farfar. He can't be anywhere else," said Stella, desperation had crept into her voice.

They searched everywhere, among the sparse suitcases and few skis, behind ski boot bags and large sacks of other equipment. But the polar bear had vanished.

"We have to search the other side of the train," said Stella, pulling at her grandpa's sleeve. "We must have missed him when we came back from the restaurant."

They headed back towards the front of the train, again scanning every open berth. Soon they were opposite their own one again when they saw someone coming towards them.

The ticket collector! Stella gripped her grandpa's arm and whispered, "Farfar, it's him, he's the one who took Max."

Her grandpa stopped in his tracks not quite sure if they should confront the ticket collector or slip back into their berth. But before he could do anything the ticket collector was standing in the corridor blocking their way.

"Can I be of any help?" he asked, his face looking redder than before.

"We were just returning to our berth," replied Gustav, pulling at the handle and pushing the door inward. The door did not budge.

"Are you having trouble getting into your own

berth? Sometimes the door cards can be a bit tricky," said the ticket collector. A curt and polite smile was playing on his lips, but Stella noticed that his eyes were cold and piercing.

He pulled out a card from his inside pocket and slipped it into the slot of the door, pulled down the handle and pushed the door open. He peeped in before moving to the side to let Stella and her grandpa in.

"Hmm, thank you for your help," replied Gustav, slightly taken aback, and feeling somehow compelled to obey.

Stella stepped into the berth before her grandpa, giving a hard tug at his sleeve. He followed her in and closed the door on the ticket collector, who was still smiling and watching them.

"He's got the card to get into our berth," hissed Stella under her breath.

"Of course, he has," replied Gustav, also whispering, "all the railway staff should be able to access the sleepers, Stella, they work on the train."

"He could have opened the door and taken Max. Remember how suspicious he was of your sneezing fit? I bet he came snooping around when we were in the restaurant car." Stella's tone was more urgent and her forehead scrunched up.

Her grandpa shook his head and sat down with a sigh on his bed. "No Stella, I'm sure he didn't, did you see how he tried to look inside again. He was obviously still curious to see if we had something to hide."

Stella sat down frowning deeply. "Yes, I suppose you're right, Farfar. Why would he want to look in if he had already taken Max?"

They both sat there staring, eyes wide thinking of what to do next. Stella threw herself back on the bed onto her soft bag where mummintroll and pippi were still stuffed. She had not taken them out yet. Her head hit something hard, then it moved. She sat up again with a start and held on to her grandpa. A black nose and white face appeared, and a pair of sleepy black eyes peered at them. Then Max yawned, his pink tongue curling up comically.

"Max!" yelped Stella in delight, picking up the warm and soft cuddly ball of fur. "You naughty, naughty cub, you scared us to bits," she scolded stroking him tenderly and rubbing her cheek on his head.

"Here we were looking all over for you, thinking you had been kidnapped again," said Gustav, his watery eyes twinkling, "and you had crept back into your favorite bag."

Stella nodded happily to her grandpa. "He really likes his soft bag. He feels safe and cozy sleeping with mummintroll and Pippi. How silly of me. Why didn't I think of looking there for him?"

"He's so well hidden among the other two toys, you'd have to know he was there to spot him," added Stella.

"He is indeed," replied Gustav nodding, "it's a suitable place to hide Max. But it won't last long. Max is getting bigger every day, soon, you won't be able to hide him there any longer.

Gustav looked at Stella, his eyes full of concern. "In fact, Stella soon, you won't be able to look after him at all."

Stella did not reply. She cuddled Max and held him closer, choosing to ignore her grandpa for the time being.

Chapter Glossary

Raggmunk-Swedish potato cakes

Princesstårta (Princess cake) - a thin layer of vibrantly green marzipan crowned with a pink rose conceals the dome of fluffy cream resting on a minimal layer of fruit filling, custard, and sponge cake.

Chapter Questions

1. Which toilets did the ticket collector want Stella to use?
2. What did Stella order that was her favorite?
3. What was Gustav's ideas for what happened to max?
4. Where was max found?

CHAPTER NINE

THE ICE HOTEL

Stella opened her eyes. Someone was rocking her bed. Were they trying to wake her up? What time was it? Where was she?

"Sofi? Is that you?" she murmured still half asleep.

Then it struck her. The fog in her head cleared. They were on the train heading towards the Ice Hotel and

Max was with them too. Sofi was not, she thought with a bit of guilt.

She sat up in the small but comfortable bed and leant over the top to search for Max. There he was, curled up in the soft bag. It was obvious he loved the bag, and it had officially become his hideout. Every time Stella put him on the bed, he would crawl back into the bag.

Now that she knew about his favorite place, she would know where to look for him the next time he went missing, and not panic as she had done the night before.

She could hear her grandpa's soft snores from below. She did not want to wake him up, but from the window, she could see the faint morning light creeping up over the horizon. They were due to arrive in Kiruna at around eight thirty and she was sure it was at least past seven thirty.

As if on cue there was a soft knock on the door.

"Pappa, Stella, time to get up and get dressed," came Alexander's voice from behind the door.

Stella flung the duvet off her and scrambled down the rungs in case her father decided to come in. Although Max was well hidden in the bag, he might wake up and make one of his funny noises.

"Getting up pappa," Stella whispered from behind the door."

"Good, we'll be in Kiruna in thirty minutes. We just have time for a quick breakfast," came Alexander's reply.

When they pulled into the station of Kiruna half an hour later and stepped onto the platform Stella was still dizzy with sleep. The train station reminded her of a place you would find in a fantasy book. The roof of the small red-brick station house was loaded with snow, and the lone icy platform was slippery. Passengers were getting off the train and dragging bags and skis towards the small exit.

With Max concealed in the bag, Gustav was carrying, Stella and her family followed the other passengers into the small waiting area and out through the station's main entrance.

"The bus stop is a bit further down," said Alexander walking towards what looked like the center of the village. He was carrying their cross-country skis enclosed in a large ski bag and two additional heavy bags. He hushed Emma's protests when she insisted on carrying something too.

Stella followed her father, her own backpack on her back. When they walked through the small town, she felt as if they had stepped into another world. They were so far from the modern buildings and the traffic in Stockholm. Here in Lapland time seemed to have frozen in with the landscape. Only peace and beauty reigned, the ugliness of the city belonged to another land.

They were soon on the bus heading towards Jukkasjarvi and the Ice hotel.

"How far is it to the Ice hotel," asked Stella fidgeting in the seat next to her grandpa.

"Not far at all," replied Alexander from the seat in front of Stella, "half an hour at the most."

Stella was worried Max would wake up and try to get out of the bag. For the moment, he was asleep in the soft bag that was tucked between Stella and her grandpa. They had fed Max and she had played with him before getting off the train. So, Stella hoped for the best.

When the bus left Kiruna the open land stretched for miles and miles towards the ice blue horizon. The spruce trees were draped in snow, and the branches hung low under its weight. The lower ones reached right to the ground and merged in with the snow.

The deep blue sky was immense and streaked with thin layers of clouds that reached across towards the mountain tops in the distance. The sun was still low in the mountain range, so only a pale light hung over the magical scenery.

"It's beautiful," sighed Stella, her face pressed to the window.

Gustav nodded, also lost in awe at Lapland's beauty.

"It's been a while since I was up in these regions," said Gustav, "it feels like coming home in a way."

Gustav had worked for years up in the Lapland as a forest agent for the Swedish Forestry department and was a passionate outdoor man.

"This is also a delightful home for our little friend," he added in a whisper.

Stella simply nodded, without turning her gaze from the landscape. She did not want to think of what they were to do about Max, she wanted to play with him and look after the cub. She was sure she could cope perfectly well without anyone's help.

"Look," exclaimed Alexander pointing behind them. "Can you see the sledges drawn by reindeer over there?"

Stella squinted across the expanse of snow and could just make out a train of animals pulling something behind them.

"Are those really reindeer?" she exclaimed. "I mean real wild reindeer?"

"Yes of course," answered Gustav with a chuckle. "Although not exactly wild anymore. Those driving them are the Sami people and they tame the reindeer and use them for transport, fur and meat."

Stella turned around to face her grandpa. "Are those the Lapland people you told me about Farfar?"

"Yes, the very ones," he replied. "They're indigenous to these regions. They dress in bright royal blue costumes embroidered with yellow and red. They are reindeer herders and nomadic people, at least thcy were many decades ago. Now, most of them go around in snowmobiles, and the sledges are for tourists like you and me."

"Oh," said Stella looking out of the window again, "that's sad. I would much prefer to go in a sledge with reindeer."

The bus slowed down as it drew alongside a frozen river. Stella spotted a few scattered wood huts with snow piled on the roofs. A snowmobile zoomed past in the opposite direction. A church came into view, painted red and white in the typical Swedish style, and one or two Sami women with large baskets in their arms walked past it.

As the bus entered the village, Stella saw a signpost with 'Jukkasjärvi' on it, and in the distance, she noticed a strange blueish hue. "What is that?" she asked a puzzled frown on her brow.

"That, Stella is the Ice hotel," replied Gustav.

Stella's mouth dropped as the bus turned the corner and pulled up into a roundabout then stopped with a whoosh. She stared, transfixed at the amazing sight before her.

The building, if it could be called as such, had a peculiar domed shaped front with a slightly pointed top. The large entrance door seemed to be made of dark tainted glass and reflected the blue-hued ice around it. Beside the main building were other domed shaped or square buildings that formed a complex of bungalow like lodgings.

But what was amazing about them was that all of them, absolutely all, were made from ice.

"Are these buildings really made of ice only?" asked Stella still transfixed by the scene.

"Every single one of them," replied Gustav. "And not only the exterior. The interior, with its tables, beds, steps, bars. Everything is made from ice."

"But how do they do it Farfar?" went on Stella still too amazed to realize that what she was looking at was real.

"They cut out blocks of ice every year at the beginning of winter and start rebuilding the main area. Then, they add on the sleeping sections throughout the months, until they finish it completely by the end of December," explained Gustav.

"What?" exclaimed Stella amazed. "Do you mean they build the Ice hotel every year repeatedly?"

"Oh yes, of course, they do. The ice melts after the winter," replied Gustav amused at Stella's amazement.

"But it's enormous how can they build this ice palace in such an abbreviated time?" Stella went on.

"It is enormous," said Gustav, "but there are lots of men working on the hotel. They cut more than three thousand tons of ice from the Torne River. The rest is made of snow, which they gather from the landscape. Just imagine Stella, they need ten times more snow than ice. So, it's quite a job every year."

The passengers started getting off the bus, but Stella sat there staring at the blue-tinged front entrance. It looked so ethereal that Stella expected it to disappear at any moment. Gustav gently pulled at Stella's arm to get her moving, and together they stepped onto the large area of compact snow in front of the hotel's entrance.

Stella followed her father, mother and grandpa in through the dark glass doors. They entered an enormous domed shaped hall with ice sculptures in every corner of the large ice area. A large arc-shaped reception area lit from underneath with blueish lights was placed at the far end of the hall. It reminded Stella of a spaceship about to take off.

There was an enormous chandelier made of ice crystals hanging from the center of the ceiling and it glittered like thousands of stars. The whole area was so breathtaking that Stella could not move, too struck with the sight. Every corner, every piece of furniture and object was made of ice.

"Here we are family!" announced Alexander waving two key cards he had just picked up at the reception desk. "Stella and Farfar you have a room for you two and Emma and I have a room further down. Follow me everyone."

Stella followed down the ice sculpted corridors and past art objects made of ice. She was also wondering how they would ever sleep in such a cold place without freezing.

She soon found the answer the moment she stepped into their room. The beds were sculpted in ice and draped with reindeer skins. There were also funny looking balls of snow decorating the room, these reminded Stella of large white Christmas ornaments.

Stella went over to the reindeer skins and lifted them to see what kind of mattress they would be sleeping on.

Meanwhile, Gustav put down the bag where Max was sleeping and came over to Stella. "Under these reindeer skins are spruce mattresses. These are specially made to insulate us from the cold of the ice. While these extra thick sleeping bags will keep us warm all through the night."

"How cold is it in here Farfar" asked Stella.

"Minus five degrees. It can't get any warmer or the ice would melt. But don't worry Stella," he added with a grin, "they do have a warm area to store our clothes in, and even a sauna."

The bag stirred and Max's black nose sniffed the air. Stella jumped down from the ice bed and swept the bear in her arms. "You'll love this place, Max," said Stella in glee. "It's just perfect for you. We'll go skiing, sledging, and spend all day playing in the snow."

Stella turned to her grandpa and pleaded, "Farfar,

can we go now, please? I can't wait to take Max into the snow. We can put on our cross-country skis and visit the woods. He'll love that."

"Come on you two in there," came Alexander's voice from outside the room. "Emma and I are heading to the sauna and swimming pool. We need to relax after such a long journey. We'll meet you at the pool."

Stella's eyes suddenly took on a deep and troubled expression. She started to tremble a little, but not from the cold. "Not the pool please," she pleaded. Gustav went over to Stella and took her into his arms.

"It's alright Stella, I'll stay with you and Max. We'll go and have lots of fun in the snow. Let the old people laze about in the pool. The three of us have better things to do. I'll talk to your father." He gave her an encouraging wink and a big hug.

Stella looked into her grandpa's eyes, an expression of relief lit up her face. She nodded gratefully and her smile crept back, the feeling of dread slowly slipping away. Stella was terrorized of water.

Chapter glossary

Kiruna - last station before Jukkasjarvi the Ice hotel.

Chapter questions

1. What did Gustav do for a living?
2. What is a typical dress for the Lapland people?
3. What is he building process for the ice hotel?
4. How much ice is needed for the ice hotel?
5. What is used to keep warm on the ice beds?

CHAPTER TEN

DAY IN THE LAPLAND

Stella and her grandpa left their luxury room to explore the palace of ice. She marveled at the sparkling walls and ceilings, the bizarrely shaped corners and the works of art in every recess.

Stella had popped Max in the bag again with Mumintroll, but she could see that he was not asleep. His small white ears and black nose popped out and peered around in curiosity.

They walked through the labyrinth of blue ice and crystal brilliant corridors. It reminded Stella of the film Frost and the princess' kingdom of eternal winter. They cut across the large entrance hall, the snow crunching beneath their feet, and past the ice bar. The seats were sculpted in snow and draped with reindeer skins. People sat sipping their colorful drinks from glasses made of ice.

Stella noticed that a crowd had gathered around a large arched entrance, and she wondered what was happening.

"What's are all those people doing around there Farfar?"

Gustav shook his head and looked as puzzled as Stella. "I have no idea, but let's go and have a peep," he said.

They moved closer to the group of people gathered outside a large opening. Gustav stretched his neck to get a better view. He then smiled and looked down at Stella.

"What is it Farfar?" asked Stella frustrated she could not see over the people's heads.

"See for yourself," he said with a twinkle in his eye and lifted Stella's light frame above the heads.

Stella's jaw dropped in amazement. Before her eyes

was the most enchanting sight she had ever laid eyes on. There in a large a cavernous room stood a young woman dressed as a princess. Her long sweeping white lace dress sparkled in silver. She stood majestically beside a tall blond man, he too, dressed in a creamy white suit. They were facing each other and looking blissful as they held hands in front of a large transparent block of ice, like a church altar.

"An ice wedding," exclaimed Gustav.

"Wow, it's amazing" gasped Stella. "I bet mamma would have loved to get married in here."

"It's never too late you know Stella. Maybe one day your father will ask your mother to marry him again," said Gustav with a grin.

"Can you get married twice?" asked Stella with a frown.

"Of course, you can," replied Gustav chuckling, "It's fun to celebrate when a couple is so in love. I should have married your grandma every year when I had a chance," he added dropping Stella back down to the ground and turning his head to hide the tears in his eyes.

Stella felt sad for her grandpa. She knew how much he missed his wife. She had died when Stella was only four. That was probably another reason he had moved in with them, as well as having to help look after Stella.

"Come on let's go skiing," said Gustav trying to sound cheerful again.

Stella nodded and gave her grandpa a hug. "Let's go Farfar. It's time Max had a run in the snow."

They donned their boots and furry hats and headed towards the back entrance of the Ice hotel to get the skis from the deposit area. There were cross-country tracks leading towards the woodlands and mountains just outside the hotel.

Stella and her grandpa strapped on their skis and pushed away from the hotel to get away from curious eyes. When they were at a safe distance, Gustav let Max out of the bag. Max was restless to get out, and as soon as Gustav dropped the bag he toppled over onto the snow and sniffed the air in delight.

"He loves it!" exclaimed Stella.

"Of course, he does. It's his real home here," replied Gustav with a laugh.

They moved on in the snow, slowly at first because Max kept toppling over. He was less clumsy in the snow than on slippery floors, as he could get a better grip with his claws. The snow was very deep and soft but in some areas, it was hard, due to the Lapland's freezing temperatures. In these parts the world, the snow's surface froze rapidly after a mild spell.

"Keep right on the tracks Stella and you'll be perfectly safe," said Gustav, as he moved forward with ease.

"Come on Max run," cried out Stella, pushing on her poles and gliding along behind her grandpa. Max plodded along clumsily until Gustav picked him up and placed him on his two skis just in front of his straps. He kept his skis together and moved along just by pushing with his poles, and off he glided along with Max.

Stella burst out laughing as she watched her grandpa and Max. The little bear was sniffing the air and looking as comfortable as if he were sitting on the lounge sofa.

They spent the morning exploring the woods, skiing and having snowball fights until they were exhausted. They even had fun falling into the snow and making snow angels. Stella was enjoying herself so much, she hardly noticed the cold snow that slipped into her neck. But soon her stomach started to grumble.

"Let's go back for a yummy fika," declared Gustav,

who was also getting hungry.

Stella's mouth watered and her stomach grumbled again at the thought of the popular Swedish teatime snack. It was one of her favorite moments of the day, especially because they did not always have time for a fika during her school week. But when they did, they would settle down at home or at a coffee or pastry shop, and tuck into cakes, tea or lemonade in the best of Swedish traditions.

By the time, they got back to the Ice hotel Max was already asleep in the bag again. They left him on the reindeer skins in their ice-bedroom and went off to look for Emma and Alexander. They found them in the ice sculpting room, where Emma was trying to make her own work of ice art. She had a chisel in her hand and was busy chipping off the ice from a block, frowning in concentration. Stella took a closer look and her eyes widened.

"That looks like Sofi," she exclaimed. Stella felt a bit of guilt again. She had completely forgotten about her pet back at home. They had left Sofi with the neighbors, who were looking after her over the weekend.

"It is!" exclaimed Emma with a satisfied smile. "So, I haven't wasted nearly two hours sculpting away if I've at least managed to get a slight resemblance to our family pet."

"They say that ice sculpting is relaxing," added Alexander and Mr. Nord the master sculptor over there is very clever."

"Oh yes," added Emma, "I've really enjoyed this experience, so much so that I think I'll start wood sculpting when we get back home."

Stella nodded enthusiastically. She was so happy to see her mother in such good spirits and with a renewed energy.

"Stella and I are famished and we wanted to go for a fika," said Gustav.

"Excellent idea," said Alexander. "I know, why don't we go into the old town of Jukkasjärvi and have a traditional fika in one of the lovely cafés. Then we can go and visit the Sami village where you can get close to the reindeer. We can also taste their food and who knows try driving a sledge with real reindeer at the head."

Stella hugged her father and started fidgeting around the ice sculpting studio. All she wanted to do now was to get back outdoors. She was fretting to explore the village and the fascinating Sami people and get up close to a real reindeer.

Soon they were sitting in a warm café sipping hot drinks. Spread before them on the red and white embroidered tablecloth was a platter with a selection of delicious pastries. Stella loved the Rulltårta, which was a roll cake filled with jam and cream and cut into slices. She also tasted the kanelbullar, which were cinnamon buns sprinkled with pearl sugar. She thought she would even try the delicious looking Chocolate balls, but by then she was so full she thought she would burst.

"I've never had such a delicious fika in my life," she exclaimed when she had finished the last crumbs on her plate and emptied her cup of hot cocoa.

"Where do you put all that cake?" asked Gustav blinking at Stella in astonishment.

"Are you sure you don't have a polar bear under the table who's helping you with your fika cake?" he winked at Stella who opened her eyes wide at him.

"Come on everyone," said Alexander getting up from the table, "let's go and visit the Sami tents and look at their lovely craft work, and the reindeer of course."

When Stella walked out into the late afternoon air the cold bit at her nose and stung her eyes. She remembered the freezer temperature at home, and she was sure it was close to -17 if not more.

They crunched along on the snow through the village until they reached the far end where large tents were sheltered under spruce trees. Bright lights lit the tents from the inside and Stella could see silhouettes moving about. She could also smell a delicious aroma of stew filtering out from the inside.

"Hmm, that smells good," said Stella.

"Yes, it does," replied Gustav, "it's the traditional reindeer stew the Sami people love to eat."

Although Stella had to admit it smelled delicious she was not sure she could eat reindeer meat. She suddenly spotted a white and grey one with a brightly colored harness just outside one of the tents.

"Oh, look at the reindeer," exclaimed Stella heading towards the animal. "Look how furry his neck is and what big antlers he has."

They all came closer to the tents. A Sami appeared from the far-left tent. She had a thick royal blue costume with yellow and red embroidery along the collar and buttons. She was also wearing a fur hat lined with the same bright embroidered lining.

She gestured to Stella and her family to follow her

into the tent. Stella led the way timidly behind the old woman. As she stepped inside the delicious aroma grew more intense.

It was surprisingly warm inside the tent. Reindeer skins were strewn over low beds, like the ones at the Ice hotel. A large black pot, which reminded Stella of a witch's cauldron, hung over glowing embers. Stella's nostrils flared at the intense and mouth-watering smell of the delicious stew. She had just had a hearty fika and she was not hungry, but the smell was appetizing nonetheless.

In the tent were a younger woman and a man with two children, who looked younger than Stella. One of them was wearing a fur hat, with the ear flaps turned up from the ears. They all looked comfortable, well fed and happy. Their smiles were friendly and welcoming.

"Will you stay for dinner with us?" asked the old Sami woman with twinkling eyes.

"That's very nice of you to ask, but we've just had our fika, and we couldn't eat anything else," replied Alexander, with a smile.

Stella was amazed at how hospitable these Sami people were, and was sorry they had to leave.

"Can't we go and visit them again please pappa,"

she pleaded, when they left the tent and walked back to the Ice hotel.

Alexander noticed how let down Stella was. "What we can do is come over tomorrow before we go to see the Northern lights, we only have two days and lots of things to do."

Stella felt suddenly exhausted as they headed back to the hotel. She could hardly keep her eyes open and doubted she would manage any dinner. However, the adventure was not over yet.

When they stepped into the reception area there was a group of people gathered around the ice bar and Stella's father headed towards them. Stella wondered what he was up to, when a man stood up and announced, "is everyone ready for the survival tour?"

Stella looked up at her grandpa with eyes wide with puzzlement.

"The survival tour?" she whispered.

Her grandpa smiled and lifted his shoulders. "Well, I suppose it's not easy to sleep at -5 degrees, so we have to be aware of a few important things if we don't want to freeze tonight."

Stella nodded slowly. Something was rattling at in

her mind. "Do you think Max will be alright?"

"Oh, he'll be just fine. He'll be the happiest of us all," answered Gustav with a wink.

The man leading the survival tour told the group what they should wear in their thermal sleeping bag. He also gave suggestions about getting as much heat as they could from the thick bag.

"Once you have collected the blue thermal sleeping bag from the reception head to your rooms. Lay the sleeping bag on the reindeer skins and unzip it without opening it. Next, take off your boots and place them beside your bed ready for the morning. Remember, don't step on the ice with your feet, you must avoid getting them damp!"

Stella was listening carefully. It sounded fun to her, although some people around her had worried expressions.

The man from the hotel staff went on. "Next, quickly undress leaving only your thermal underwear on, and your hat and scarf. Roll up your outer clothing and stuff them at the bottom of your sleeping bag. The less you wear the warmer you will be throughout the night. Quickly scramble into the sleeping bag like this."

The man then got into the sleeping bag and wriggled right into it. He then gathered it up to his armpits and zipped up the bag. Next, he slotted himself right in and buried himself deep inside pulling it right over his hat. He looked as if he was dancing about as he wriggled to get in, burying himself deep into the warm sack. There were a few laughs as he demonstrated the process and Stella giggled too.

"It looks like he's getting ready for a potato bag race," Stella chuckled, anticipating the sleeping bag ritual with excitement.

Once the demonstration was over, the guests were offered cold and hot drinks.

"Try and avoid drinking before you settle for the night," added their hotel guide.

"Why can't we drink?" asked Stella.

"You really want to avoid getting out of the sleeping bag during the night to pee," said Alexander, "it could get very uncomfortable. He's also referring to alcoholic drinks. They can increase heat loss, and that is definitely something you want to avoid in these conditions."

Stella nodded. All she wanted to do now was get into the funny looking sleeping bag and curl up to sleep. Her eyelids felt very heavy.

Chapter Glossary

Rulltårta - Roll Cake- a sponge cake, baked in a big rectangle, then filled with something delicious (like whipped cream and jam), then rolled and cut into slices.

Kanelbullar - Cinnamon Buns - the most iconic of the fika recipes. The dough is spiced with a little cinnamon, which is what makes for the distinct Swedish cinnamon bun taste.

Fika - Typical Swedish tea with cakes coffee, tea and juice.

Sami People - Indigenous people from the Lapland

Chapter Questions

1. What did the walk through the ice remind Stella of?
2. What did Stella see that she thought was amazing?
3. How old was Stella when her grandmother died?
4. What did Stella and max do for fun outside?
5. What smell did Stella find delicious?
6. What was important to know about survival procedures?

CHAPTER ELEVEN

STELLA GETS CROSS WITH FARFAR

Stella opened her eyes to an intense icy blue. She huddled up in her warm cocoon and yawned. Mist clouded around her as her breath met with the icy air and turned into a dewy halo.

When entering their ice room, the night before, Stella had doubted she would ever be able to sleep. After all, it was below zero. But once she had slipped into the thermal sleeping bag she soon found warmth and comfort.

Stella had closed her eyes and imagined she was in a glacier cave like in the ancient times. She guessed that there were no special sleeping bags then and was relieved she had her own. Then she had slipped into a deep sleep.

A strange croaking noise had woken her up. She recognized Max's call for food. He was sniffing the air beside Stella's bed, but she was not sure she wanted to get out of the warm sleeping bag to feed him. Taking care of a Polar bear cub was not easy, she had to admit, but she would manage.

Stella unzipped the thickly padded bag and immediately the cold air grasped around her feet and hands.

"Brrr," shivered Stella. But before she could get into her warm outdoor clothes a ringing bell sounded from outside the door. Stella scrambled out of her sleeping bag and lifted Max up into her arms. She pushed him into the sleeping bag and snuggled in to hide him. Stella then looked over to her grandpa who was also awake and nodded.

Gustav nodded back and growled, "Come in."

"Good morning guests," said a young woman wearing a hat, boots and scarf. She entered their room holding a large metal jug.

"Here is your hot Lingonberry juice, and as soon as you have finished drinking we'll be waiting for you for a hot sauna followed by breakfast."

She then poured the hot red liquid into two large mugs and set them next to Stella's and Gustav's bed.

Stella was wiggling in the sleeping bag trying to stop Max from getting out. The lady smiled at her and said, "I hope you're not getting cold in there?"

Stella shook her head without a word, and Gustav came to the rescue. "We're nice and warm in here, but I think we may both need to get to the toilet."

He smiled at the woman, who got the hint and left the room adding that they could come for a sauna whenever they wanted.

The moment she left the room, Max jumped out of the sleeping bag and went sliding across the icy floor. Stella burst out laughing. The cub slid all the way to Gustav's bed and bumped his head against the ice step, he shook himself vigorously and sniffed the air again.

"He's grown since we left," mused Gustav as they both stared at Max from the comfort of their warm sleeping bags. Stella's grandpa was sitting up, the sleeping bag still over his head, sipping the hot delicious brew.

"He hardly fits in your soft bag Stella, and he'll soon need substantial food," he added with a frown, putting down his cup.

Stella's stomach filled with butterflies. She had a foreboding that her grandpa was about to tell her something she did not want to hear.

"Stella," started Gustav, clearing his throat, "We have to find a solution for Max and we're in the right place to find a home for him. I'll have to do some tracking today, see if there's a possibility to find a home for Max."

"But...but Farfar...he's too little, he still needs me to look after him. He won't survive out there alone in the wilderness," said Stella, her voice full of desperation.

"Stella, listen. Soon, he won't be little any longer. Look at him, he's too big to hide now. You can't keep disguising him. He needs to be free to roam around. He'll soon be eating more and more, and not just the milk preparation we give him," he paused and looked over to Stella.

She lowered her eyes and looked away, a tear was running down her cheek.

"And Stella," he went on, "he's a wild animal, he'll

soon become dangerous, even though he may love you."

"But I can teach him, tame him, just like I did with Sofi!" she interjected, now turning her eyes towards her grandpa.

Gustav shook his head; his eyes were full of concern as he looked into his granddaughter's desperate eyes. Stella looked away again.

She unzipped her sleeping bag and reached down to the bottom for her clothes, quickly slipping them on. Then she climbed out of the sack and put on her boots. She ignored the hot Lingonberry juice and went over to Max who was busy biting at his soft white fur. He looked up at Stella and twitched his small round ears and his little black nose. Stella wrapped her arms around him and buried her face in the woolly neck. Max licked Stella's pixie ears and she giggled with delight.

"Come here Max, Stella will feed you now, then we'll go out and have some fun on the skis again. You love that don't you," said Stella cheering up again at the prospect of another adventure on the snow with Max.

Gustav shook his head under the sleeping bag. His eyes anxious as he watched Stella feeding Max. He finally finished his brew and got dressed in a hurry to avoid freezing.

"Come on Stella let's go to the sauna and then for our breakfast," he said trying to sound joyful for Stella's sake.

"Oh, I hope we don't have to go to the swimming pool after," said Stella, her eyes filled with fear.

"Swimming pool? Who wants to go swimming when there's a scrumptious breakfast waiting for us after the sauna," said Gustav with a large smile.

He wanted to avoid getting Stella anxious and worried again. Stella was terrified of water. Although her parents and her grandpa had tried to help her overcome her fear, she still cringed if someone suggested going for a swim.

Stella suddenly felt terribly hungry. She got up leaving Max curled up on the reindeer skins, happily filled up with his breakfast and followed her grandpa out of the ice room towards the sauna.

Gustav paused outside the door and hung up the 'do not disturb' sign.

"We don't want anyone disturbing Max's sleep, do we?" he said with a wink.

There was so much to choose from at the hotel's

buffet. With different kinds of bread, cereals, porridge, yoghurt, fruit and berries, loads of juices, cheese, ham, eggs, bacon, salmon and even pancakes to Stella's delight. She had never seen anything like it. Luckily the restaurant was in the warm part of the hotel.

After a full breakfast, Stella and her grandpa headed out with Max on their skis towards the forest and Lake Sautusjärvi, a large lake, which was not far from the Ice hotel. The morning was crisp and cold. So, cold that the air seemed to be filled with tiny crystal-like particles.

"This is perfect weather for us to watch the Northern night show this evening," said Gustav as he panted along on his skis his breath turning into ice clouds.

"I can't wait, Farfar," said Stella picking up speed as she thought about the incredible spectacle they would see tonight. The halo of ghost-like green and pink lights was probably the eeriest and most fascinating experience anyone could ever witness.

"If we're lucky we may also be able to see violet and red lights too, although that's rare to see. You just wait and see Stella, it's one of the most amazing sights I've ever seen, and your Farfar has seen lots of things in his life."

Max was hopping along easily. He had quickly

adapted to his natural habitat and was having just as much fun as Stella.

They finally reached the border of the lake, which was now a huge expanse of ice and snow.

"Do people go ice skating here Farfar? “asked Stella, feeling the urge to ice skate too.

"Oh yes, it's a great place to come," replied Gustav, "But you need to be careful. In some places, the ice is thin, especially at the end of the winter, although that depends on the year and on how cold the winter has been."

"But we can't stop here, today we're heading on an expedition Stella," added Gustav.

Stella stopped in her ski tracks. "We are?" she asked excited at the prospect and wondering what it could possibly be.

Her grandpa stopped too and came beside her on his skis. "Yes. It's time to go looking for Leo," he announced solemnly.

"Leo?" said Stella her eyes wide in amazement, "you mean your Leo, the polar bear you met eight years ago? But why should we be looking for Leo? And how do you know he's still here?"

Her grandpa looked across the lake and towards the

woods beyond. "I'm sure he is Stella; I can feel he is." Gustav's eyes were intensely blue as he scrutinized the horizon, that Stella had no doubt he was right. Her stomach fluttered and she felt anxious. She waited for her grandpa to go on.

"I need to ask Leo to look after Max," said Gustav finally. Stella swallowed hard. She found it hard to talk. Her heart started beating fast. She knew deep down that her grandpa was right, but she felt betrayed by him. Her grandpa was not his usual self, playful and childlike. He was behaving like all the other adults. Pretending he was happy to have Max but deep down he was scheming to get rid of him.

Stella's anger rose. Her best friend Farfar was betraying her. In fact, she was fuming. She would not help her grandpa look for Leo. Never. She wanted to be by herself now. She and Max would play as best friends. She could not rely on her grandpa, what would he come up with next.

"I'm getting cold," she said, her voice trembling slightly. "I'm going back to the hotel. You go and look for your polar bear. I'll stay with mine."

And without another word she flung her skis over

and headed back in the opposite direction, with Max toppling along behind her.

Gustav's pained expression followed his granddaughter's movements as she headed back towards the hotel. He knew it was going to be hard to convince Stella to part with Max, but it was the only sensible solution. That or take him back to the zoo, which was something he did not want to do. He turned around and looked over the lake again to the forest.

Chapter Glossary

Sautusjärvi Lake: Large lake near the Ice hotel.

Typical Swedish Breakfast: flavors are generally mild; bread, coffee and a bowl with yoghurt or a dairy product and cereals are often found on a Swedish breakfast table, or perhaps a bowl of oatmeal porridge with fruits or berries.

Lingonberry juice: healthy antioxidant juice made from lingonberries or side of the bed for easy access.

Chapter Questions

1. What woke up Stella?
2. Where did Stella and Gustav take max on skis?
3. What do you have to watch out for while ice skating?
4. What is Gustav's plan when he finds Leo?

C H A P T E R T W E L V E

MAX AND STELLA GET INTO TROUBLE

Stella was still fuming when she spotted the Ice hotel in the distance. She felt cornered and alone. Her grandpa had betrayed her trust and was not being her true friend as he usually was.

"I don't want to go back to the hotel," she said out loud to Max, " who cares about Farfar, we can have fun by ourselves."

She had stopped skiing and was looking at Max who was sitting in the snow, panting. His bright pink tongue a splash of color in contrast with the white of his fur and the snow.

"Why don't we go ice skating," she blurted out with excitement, "yes, that would be really fun. I need to teach you how to walk on ice because that's where you will be living in a few years' time. When you are ready for the wildlife of course," she added as if to make things clear with anyone who dared to contradict her.

Stella traced her tracks back to the deposit area at the back of the hotel, where all the skis and sledges were stored. She hoped they would not meet anyone around there, as she was not sure she would be able to carry Max in the bag by herself without her grandpa's help.

She had to admit that he was getting rather heavy and too big for the bag. But she soon dismissed the problem when she saw that there was no one about.

"Everyone's probably skiing or sledging or snow-shoeing," said Stella as she quickly unlatched her skis and opened the big blue bag in which her father had stored the ice skates.

"Here they are," said Stella, "I'll keep my ski shoes

on, they're comfortable enough. I don't want to risk going inside without you," she said to Max.

No sooner had Stella closed the deposit locker door that they were both heading towards the lake again, ice skates in hand.

Although the sun was not high up above the horizon the light was dazzling white. Stella fitted her eye goggles over her eyes to protect them from the blaze. This was the time of year Stella's grandpa liked to call 'spring winter', he said it was the most beautiful time to be in the Swedish mountains. The expanse of snow twinkled brilliantly as it started to melt and freeze and the sun finally made its presence more dominating.

"I love trip skating," declared Stella, "We can only skate on the skate rinks back in Stockholm. But this is the real thing. Sliding across the natural ice. Just look at that forest around the lake, it's immense."

Stella paused to gaze ahead at the lake and trees in the distance. She could imagine the feel of gliding everywhere she wanted to, without barriers or people in her way.

She started skipping towards the lake but soon trudged along again due to the heavy snow. Max hopped by her side, nose twitching and little black eyes alert, his ears picking up at the slightest noise.

It took them a long time to reach the lake on foot and by the time they came to the spot Stella had left her grandpa standing, both she and Max were out of breath.

The area was deserted, and the wide expanse of the lake was amazingly beautiful. The blaze of the ice and the sparkling snow was breathtaking. Stella sat on a large mound of snow, which probably concealed a large log and removed her boots to put on her ice skates.

"All that walking has made me hungry," grumbled Stella, wishing she had slipped something to eat in her pocket. Her grandpa would have had something to eat or drink for sure. He always had the right things when you needed them thought Stella grudgingly.

She felt guilty now and lonely too. Max was fun but he did not have anything to say, not like her grandpa who had lots to say about everything. Stella kept having to call Max back because he wandered off and would not listen. At least Sofi always kept to Stella's heels.

"Oh well, I'm sure you'll do better than Sofi on the ice," said Stella cheering up a little.

She got up on her skates and felt slightly unsure as

her feet wobbled to one side then the other. She walked cautiously down to the lake's mantle of ice and stepped onto the surface. It felt thick and solid under her feet.

"It should be just fine," she announced to Max who followed her onto the ice and immediately slipped and fell on his bottom, sending Stella into peals of laughter.

"This is going to be fun," said Stella as she watched the cub try to get up again and fall flat on his stomach. Stella pushed off with her right skate and glided easily on the brilliant surface, then she swirled around gracefully and came back towards Max. The icy cold air and the feeling of flying over the ice sent shivers of joy through Stella's frail body. There was nothing more exhilarating than skating freely over ice.

Max was slowly mastering the slippery surface and was using his claws to keep better balance as well as using his bottom to slide a bit more gracefully. But soon he was ice skating. He hopped on the ice then fell on his stomach, sliding with his hind legs. Then he skated with all four paws, making strange circular movements.

"This is truly amazing," gasped Stella, "you're a natural ice skater Max!"

Stella swirled and twirled around Max as he padded

along, gracefully, often falling on his stomach and pushing along with his forepaws while his hind legs lay flat on the ice and followed his movements.

Stella could not stop laughing. Max was so comical on the ice. Although he was good, his movements were often clumsy, but he would learn fast, Stella thought. She pushed off further towards the center of the lake as fast as she could go. The cold air swooshed in the hair that had escaped past her woolen hat. The white golden strands were icy at the tips and her nose was red. Her scarf kept slipping off from over her nose as it caught the icy breeze. She skidded to a stop and looked across towards the distant forest.

Gustav was probably there now looking for his polar bear. Stella shrugged her shoulders and tried to dismiss the earlier squabble. Then she turned around to see how Max was doing.

He had vanished! She took her goggles off in case they had fogged up her view. But she still could not spot him.

"Max!" cried out Stella pulling up her goggles over her hat and skating fast towards the edge of the lake, "Max!"

Where was he? He could not have just disappeared into the ice! The ice! She thought, panicking. His weight must have broken the ice. He had been swallowed up under the surface.

"Max! Max!" cried Stella more desperately now.

She had nearly reached the spot where she had left Max when she heard a croaking sound and a splash to her left. Then she spotted his black nose, and his ears popped out from the ice. She rushed over to the crack in the ice and looked down in horror. Max had fallen through the ice and was trying to keep afloat in the icy water.

Stella's vision blurred and her breathing became erratic. She fell on her stomach as a reflex, so as not to crack more ice. She was about to reach out for Max who was clawing at the ice on the surface, trying to pull himself out of the water, but she faltered. She was terrified of the dark blue waters. The movement and the lapping of the small waves caused by Max's clawing sent her head spinning and made her feel sick.

Then Max disappeared again. A jolt of fear spurred Stella into action despite her fear, and she plunged her hand and her whole arm into the waters. The icy cold left her breathless, but she felt the cub's fur and held on to it with all her strength and tried to pull him up.

He was so heavy and would not stop wriggling about. The fur slipped from her gloved hand and she lost him for a few seconds. She plunged her other arm into the water and caught him again. When she tried to haul him up again, her body slid close to the edge of the crack until she was halfway stretched across the surface of the water.

Then Max suddenly jumped up and clawed at the edge of the ice, sending Stella off balance. She lost hold of him and tried to grab the edge but it was too late she fell head first into the glacial mass of water.

Her head felt as if thousands of needles were pricking at it, and she lost her breath as it whooshed out of her lungs compressed by the freezing water. She opened her eyes wide under the water, and for a moment caught a glimpse of Max's shadow over her, his hind paws kicking about. She felt paralyzed and winded, she floated in the blue immensity, her eyes open and glazed panic-stricken.

Her grandpa's words suddenly echoed in her head. The words she had heard many times before on those winter evenings when he told Stella about Leo the polar bear.

"Oh yes, I was scared Stella. But I couldn't leave

him there alone, I had to free him ... Leo didn't belong to me Stella, he belonged to his mother and father..."

Those words seem to send a surge of warmth into the whole of Stella's being. She had to save Max, she would overcome her silly fear of water, she was responsible for the cub. But Farfar was right, Max belonged to his mother and father, she could not look after him any longer.

Stella kicked hard with her legs, the weight of her skates was drawing her down, she waved her arms with one swift movement and managed to grasp onto Max's back. He had clawed his way half way up the side of the edge of the crack and Stella reached the side with one gloved hand but it slipped.

She tried again with her whole arm. She had one hand on Max as the other tried to get a grip on the ice. Then suddenly Max was up on the ice again. He had managed to get out! The clever cub was out and he was now lying flat on his stomach his nose pointed towards Stella his little eyes seemed to be in distress.

Stella caught on to Max's front paw with one arm then with extreme difficulty she managed to clutch on to him with her other arm. She held on to the cub for her life, and he stayed still did not move an inch as if knowing that

Stella's life depended on him. Stella felt dizzy and she started to tremble uncontrollably. She had no strength to lift herself up and she felt herself slipping back into the water.

Suddenly her whole body lifted and she thought she was flying in the water, but no she wasn't! She was flying in the air. She felt a pair of strong arms clutch firmly around her and saw her grandpa's face loom up at her in a hazy mist.

“What on earth are you doing Stella? Don’t you know you could have been killed?” Gustav said angrily. Then Gustav announced "I've found Leo Stella, I've found Max's family."

Chapter Glossary

Trip skating - a hugely popular pastime for all ages in Sweden and offers a unique way to experience the winter landscape.

Chapter Questions

1. What did Stella say she loved doing?
2. How exactly did Max skate?
3. How did Stella end up in the icy water?
4. How did Stella get out of the water?

CHAPTER THIRTEEN

THE NORTHERN LIGHTS

"You were right Farfar," murmured Stella from under the luxurious duvet of their 'warm quarters' at the Ice hotel.

Stella had no idea what had happened after her grandfather had heaved her out of the icy waters. All she knew was that now she felt warm and safe.

She opened her eyes and gazed into her grandfather's watery blue ones. He looked concerned, and Stella stared at him feeling guilty about her behavior. He was, of course, right. She could not look after Max. Very soon he would become too big and he needed to be out in the wild. How could she look after him if she could barely look after herself?

She frowned as if reprimanding herself, and was about to tell her grandfather that he was right about Max, when she felt a soft hand on her own.

"Stella, you gave us such a fright," Emma's voice reached Stella's heart.

Stella was relieved she had not mentioned the polar cub. Max was nowhere to be seen, her grandfather had obviously managed to keep him a secret still.

"Oh mama," said Stella, "I promise I'll learn to swim as soon as we get back to Stockholm."

She looked at her mother who came to sit on the bed next to her. Emma's lines were even deeper than usual, but as Stella spoke those words, Emma's eyes shone with renewed life. She looked up at Gustav and raised her eyebrows. He lifted his shoulders and winked at his daughter-in-law.

"After all, it is important to know how to swim. Just imagine, you could save someone's life one day, hey Stella?" said Gustav with a smile.

"Oh yes, I'm sure it would be terrible if you weren't able to save someone, just because you couldn't swim, "said Stella.

Emma shook her head, wondering what the two were going on about. She was happy her daughter had overcome her fear of water and that was what counted.

"Well, whoever you will save one day, will be very happy you decided to learn how to swim. I'm proud of you Stella and we'll go to the swimming pool as soon as we get back."

She pulled the duvet right up to Stella's chin and got up, adding, "and you know what? I'll come swimming too. But now you get some rest. We're going on a Northern Lights tour tonight, and you wouldn't want to miss that for anything in the world."

Stella's eyes lit up with excitement as she watched her mother leave the room. She did not dare to move. Her grandfather still had not uttered a word about Max. Was he angry at her? And what had happened to Max? Would he ever trust her again? Stella's stomach was in a turmoil as she waited for her grandfather to say something.

Gustav finally spoke. "You saved Max from the zoo Stella and he saved you from the icy waters. Now you are friends forever. If you love Max as much as your Farfar loves you, then you need to let him go now, Stella. The time has come to take him to his family."

Stella's heart fluttered, but she sighed with relief. She knew everything was alright again, and that her grandfather was right. She had to let her polar bear cub go, he needed a polar bear family, just like she needed her parents and her grandfather.

"Where is Max?" asked Stella realizing he was not hidden anywhere in the room.

"Oh, he's fine, I've found him an excellent hideout, while we waited for you to sleep of the fright and cold."

"Oh Farfar, can we go skiing again with Max, please, just one last time?" pleaded Stella.

Gustav's expression was still troubled as he looked at his granddaughter under the bed covers. "I'm not sure that is a good idea. You need some rest after this morning's excitement."

"Oh please, we'll go all three of us together just for

a little while. I'll be good and listen to whatever you say Farfar," she promised.

Gustav's eyes softened. "Only if you listen to your Farfar and have a gigantic fika before we go."

Stella, Gustav and Max spent the rest of the day on skis, laughing madly at Max who rolled about and jumped in the snow. He was still a bit clumsy but Stella could tell that he had a natural talent for moving about on ice and snow. She knew he did not need her to teach him. His new family would do that.

She wondered what her grandpa had been doing in the woods across the lake. She was sure he had found a way to make sure Max would be safe. He always had the right solution to everything. He was the best grandpa there was and best friend too.

After supper, that evening a group of people gathered together at the Ice Bar. Stella listened as the man with a funny looking bright blue woolen hat explained to the guests what the 'aurora borealis' was.

Stella knew this was the official name for the northern lights. She also knew that the bright lights were visible because electrically charged particles from the sun collided with the earth's atmosphere. But she listened to the man anyway.

"The auroras are created by solar winds that flow from the Sun past the Earth. These solar winds are charged with particles of ionized gas, which get drawn into our atmosphere and are pulled into the Earth's magnetic field. What happens is that as soon as they enter the atmosphere these ion particles collide with atoms high up in the air, just like tiny marbles ad release an amazing amount of energy. This energy is converted into the fantastic spectacle we can admire from this very point of the Earth. A sight that will leave you in awe," he ended dramatically.

Stella followed the group holding her father's hand, and wondering where her grandpa could possibly be. She glanced at the large clock over the reception area. There were six different clocks all showing different times in the capitals of the world. The time was now 8.30 p.m. The man had told them that if they were lucky they might start seeing the first magical lights around nine.

They walked into the clear and icy night. The sky was black and the stars twinkled merrily as if dancing on the black expanse. To Stella's surprise, there were five Sami sledges with reindeer at the head of each.

"We're going on a sledge ride?" she gasped,

squeezing her father's hand.

"Surprise!" replied Alexander, picking up Stella and dropping her into one of the sledges. They were not very big, and could take only three people as well as the Sami leading the sledge. He was standing in the front in full Sami costume, with the bright blue and red linings as well as his big furry hat, lapels covering his ears.

When Stella was settled comfortably between Alexander and Emma she suddenly remembered her grandpa again.

"Where is Farfar?" she asked not wanting to sound too anxious.

"Oh, he's being very mysterious Farfar is," replied Emma shaking her head.

"He said he would come and join us later," added Alexander, "he doesn't seem that interested in the Northern lights. Your Farfar knows these places inside out, and he's seen the aurora many times before."

Stella had her suspicions on the whereabouts of her grandpa but she was not going to share them with her parents.

They were pulled forward with a jolt, and the sledge started to slide silently on the snow. The soft pounding of the reindeer's hooves was the only sound disturbing the beautiful winter evening.

They whooshed through the frozen darkness towards the mountain that rose to the north of the Sautusjärvi lake, beyond which the forest lay dark and mysterious.

"We only have a short ride," said Alexander, as if to reassure them that the chill of the night would not be too bad, although they were covered in reindeer skins to protect them from the wind.

"If you look towards the mountain you might..." Alexander's words stopped in mid-sentence and Stella felt his hand grip hers. He was pointing with a shaky gloved hand towards the forest.

Stella's mouth dropped open and icy droplets landed on her tongue and prickled at her teeth. She could not utter one word. She was sure she was dreaming.

There over the forest the night sky had lit up with a wondrous glow. Swirling, silky lights of green and pale yellow were twisting and twirling above the canopy of fir trees.

Stella thought that was how hundreds of fairies would look like, dancing and sliding on ice, their wands leaving trails of bright green and golden magic sparks behind them.

The sledges slowed down, and a chatter of excited voices broke the magic of the mysterious and silent dancing lights.

"We're very lucky tonight," shouted the guide with the funny blue hat, "and we haven't even reached the best spot yet!"

Our Sami sledge leader shook the reins again and headed towards the mountain and the woods as the eerie green glow faded, then grew stronger, like a wave breaking on the sea shore then retreating again into the sea.

The group had nearly reached their destination when another larger wave hit the black sky. Rays of green and pink shot up like sunbeams from behind clouds. They started to ripple like thick curtains blown around by a strong draught of wind. They swayed and glowed intensely over the forest and the mountain, getting larger and larger.

Stella thought it looked very spooky. The silence and intense light were eerie. She imagined that the thunder which should have followed these lights was being trapped somewhere in the mountain, stifled, and would explode unexpectedly like a large volcano and shatter the mountain to bits.

Stella gripped onto her father and stared as if hypnotized at the glowing sky. The sledges came to a halt, and everyone got out of their cozy seats, all heads tilted towards the glowing heavens above.

Alexander took Stella by the hand and they got out too. The crowd gathered around the lake across from the forest. Here the show was so breathtaking that everyone seemed frozen in with the surrounding snow and ice.

Now, the sky was lit up with multicolored figurines which appeared to be dancing on the lake. The display of colored lights was reflected off the lake's icy surface and the whole night was ablaze with streaming purples and arcs of greens, blues, yellows, pinks and even flickers of red appeared on the outskirts.

Then, out of the eerie dancing of lights and clouds that were capturing the small group staring across the lake and up at the spectacle above, came an ever so faint noise. The reindeer's ears pricked up and the Sami turned his head and scrutinized the horizon at the base of the mountain.

The sound was similar to that of a crow croaking, and no one else paid attention except for Stella. She had recognized the sound immediately. She had heard it many times before. Max.

The reindeer fidgeted a little. They seemed nervous and the Sami man calmed them down. Now Stella knew why. They had caught the scent of a polar bear, and not only the scent of a cub's.

Stella glanced to the left towards the small mountain. The sky above it was scattered with patches of green and purple clouds. The hues were less intense than the ones over the lake. However, there was no mistaking the silhouette that was blotted against the haze of color.

A large polar bear stood far off at the base of the mountain. Stella could just make out his nose tilted upwards, as she had seen Max do so many times before, sniffing the air for food. Next to the large bear a smaller one stood, he too sniffed the air.

Tears flooded Stella's eyes as she understood what was happening. Her grandpa had found Leo and had taken Max to his new family.

Her eyes were full of tears now, and she could no longer make out the pale silhouettes. When she wiped her eyes dry, they had disappeared swallowed by the night enveloped by the rays of gleaming streamers above them.

Stella turned her head back to the light display over

the lake, her eyes brimming with tears again. Emma was watching her, a puzzled expression flickering in her eyes. They too were reflecting the green rays from the sky.

"Are you feeling alright Stella?" she asked her brow troubled.

"She's fine Emma," came a voice from behind them.

"Now everyone has a happy family and we can return home to Sofi," whispered Gustav taking Stella's hand and squeezing it.

Emma looked even more puzzled, but Stella nodded and whispered, "Yes, it's time to go back to Sofi."

Chapter Questions

1. What was the scientific name for the northern lights?
2. What exactly happens during them?
3. What did Stella think would happen after the lights stopped?
4. Who was making the sound that Stella said sounded like Max?
5. Who found Leo?
6. Who took max to Leo?
7. Did you enjoy reading this book?
8. What did you learn about this book?
9. Did all the questions frustrate you?
10. What was your favorite part of the book?
11. What about the book would you have changed?
12. What would you want to happen in part 2 of this book?

Fun Things

Facts about Sweden

- There are 9.9 million people in Sweden as of 2015
- The capital of Sweden is Stockholm
- Swedish is the official language of Sweden. The vast majority of Swedes also speak English, and generally to a very high level.
- The Swedish head of state since 1973 has been King Carl XVI Gustaf.
- Sweden is a member of the European Union, but has its own currency, the krona, or Swedish crown.
- fika – a coffee break that normally consists of coffee or tea, cookies or sweet buns, but can also include soft drinks, fruit and sandwiches.
- Lagom is an important and often-used word in Sweden. Meaning good enough, or just right, it sums up Swedish cultural and social ideals of equality and fairness.
- The country was the first in the world with freedom of the press (1766), and is at the top of global press freedom rankings.
- Sweden is one of the world's most innovative nations, and it has been called the most digitally connected economy recent Swedish inventions include Spotify and Skype
- The world's first ice hotel was built in Jukkasjärvi, Sweden, in the 1980s by architect Yngve Bergqvist. The hotel has 60 rooms and is carved out of 4,000 tons of densely packed snow and ice with occupancy available between December and April. Guests are issued thermal jumpsuits of "beaver nylon" upon check-in, and their air-lock cuffs help the wearers survive the interior temperatures as low as -8° F (-22° C).
- The northern lights, or aurora borealis, appear above the Arctic Circle (latitude 66°) and are visible around the equinoxes in late September and March and during the dark of winter in Sweden. These spectacular displays of green-blue shimmering arcs and waves of lights are

caused by solar wind, or streams of particles charged by the sun, hitting the atmosphere. The colors are the characteristic hues of different elements when they hit the plasma shield that protects Earth: blue is nitrogen and yellow-green is oxygen.

- The Oresund Bridge is the planet's longest cable-tied road, and Rail Bridge, measuring 7.8 km from Lernacken (on the Swedish side near Malmö) to the artificial island of Peberholm (Pepper Island) south of Saltholm (Salt Island) in Denmark.
- Sweden was the first country in the world to introduce standardized time, which was necessary to make understandable train tables.
- Sweden is the first country in the world with its own phone number. It connects you to a random Swede.
- Despite being a military power in the 17th century and one of the world's largest producers of weapons, Sweden has not participated in any war for almost two centuries, including both world wars

Facts About Polar Bears

The polar bear or the sea/ice bear are the world's largest land predators They can be found in the Artic, the U.S. (Alaska), Canada, Russia, Denmark (Greenland), and Norway.

Male polar bears may grow 10 feet tall and weigh over 1400 pounds. Females reach seven feet and weigh 650 pounds. In the wild polar bears live up to age 25.

A polar bear's fur is not white. Each hair is a clear hollow tube. Polar bears look white because each hollow hair reflects the light. Underneath the fur, a polar bear's skin is actually black -- the black skin soaks up the sun's heat and helps them stay warm.

Polar bears have built-in socks. The bottoms of their paws are covered with fur to keep them warm and to help with traction in slippery situations.

Polar bears huge webbed paws are perfect for cutting through the ocean at 10 kph (6 mph). Compare that to Olympic swimmers who, at best, clock in at 7 kph (4.5 mph).

Unlike brown bears, males and non-breeding females do not hibernate in the winter.

They evolved from Brown Bears more than 38 million years ago, and now there are 19 species of them known in the world.

Ice Hotel

Contact & Address
Icehotel, Marknadsvägen 63, 981 91 Jukkasjärvi, Sweden
Reception: +46 (0) 980 668 00
Email: info@icehotel.com
Book your stay
Booking dep. +46 980-66899
Our telephone service: weekdays 9 am – 4 pm
Guided tours & day visits
November, 19–April,12: daily at noon and at 4 pm.

USA Travel help to Ice Hotel

BORTON OVERSEAS
Phone: 1-800-843-0602 (toll free)
E-mail: info@bortonoverseas.com
www.bortonoverseas.com

SCANAM WORLD TOURS
Scandinavian American World Tours
Phone: 1-800-545-2204 (Toll free U.S. and Canada)
Phone: 1-609-655-1600 (tel)
www.scanamtours.com

WWF

$1 from every book sold will be donated to the World Wildlife Fund, in an effort to help protect polar bears from extinction. Should you choose to donate on your own you may do so

You can go to worldwildlife.org and print out the form and mail it to:

World Wildlife Fund

1250 Twenty-Fourth Street, N.W.

P.O. Box 97180

Washington, DC 20090-7180

Or you can call To donate by phone, call

1-800-CALL-WWF.

Or you can go online to www.worldwildlife.org

Swedish Cinnamon Buns (Kanelbullar)

Total Time 1hr 37mins

Prep 1 hr. 30 mins Cook 7 mins

Servings 6-8

Ingredients

4 teaspoons yeast
3⁄4 cup butter or 3⁄4 cup margarine
1 teaspoon salt
1 teaspoon cardamom (optional)
½ cup sugar or Swedish pearl sugar
2 cups milk
4 -5 cups flour

Directions

Melt margarine or butter.

Add milk and heat 115 F (45 C).

Dissolve yeast.

Add sugar, cardamom (optional) and salt.

Stir until mixed.

Add flour, knead into dough.

Let rise until doubled

Divide dough.

Use rolling pin to roll out large rectangle, about ¼ in. thick.

Spread with margarine, cinnamon and sugar.

Roll up into a big roll, about 2in. in diameter.

Cut ¾ in. thick slices, put onto greased cookie sheet.

Rise about 20-30 minute

Baste with whipped egg;

Add a little bit of sugar on top, or you can use some Swedish pearl sugar (available at most IKEAs or Swedish specialty stores).

Bake 450 F (225 C) about 7-10 min

Swedish Meatballs

Total Time: 55 min
Prep:30 min
Cook: 25 min
Serving size: approximately 30 meatballs, 4 to 6 servings

Ingredients

2 slices fresh white bread
1/4 cup milk
3 tablespoons clarified butter, divided
½ cup finely chopped onion
A pinch plus 1 teaspoon kosher salt
¾ lb ground chuck
¾ lb ground pork
2 large egg yolks
1/2 teaspoon black pepper
1/4 teaspoon ground allspice
1/4 teaspoon freshly grated nutmeg
¼ cup all-purpose flour
3 cups beef broth
¼ cup heavy cream

Directions

Preheat oven to 200 degrees F.

Tear the bread into pieces and place in a small mixing bowl along with the milk. Set aside.

In a 12-inch straight sided sauté pan over medium heat, melt 1 tablespoon of the butter. Add the onion and a pinch of salt and sweat until the onions are soft. Remove from the heat and set aside.

In the bowl of a stand mixer, combine the bread and milk mixture, ground chuck, pork, egg yolks, 1 teaspoon of kosher salt, black pepper, allspice, nutmeg, and onions. Beat on medium speed for 1 to 2 minutes.

shape the meatballs into round 1 ounce balls

Heat the remaining butter in the sauté pan over medium-low heat, or in an electric skillet set to 250 F. Add the meatballs and sauté until golden brown on all sides, about 7 to 10 minutes. Remove the meatballs to an ovenproof dish using a slotted spoon and place in the warmed oven.

Once all the meatballs are cooked, decrease the heat to low and add the flour to the pan or skillet. Whisk until lightly browned, approximately 1 to 2 minutes. Gradually add the beef stock and whisk until sauce begins to thicken. Add the cream and continue to cook until the gravy reaches the desired consistency. Remove the meatballs from the oven, cover with the gravy and serve.

Traditional Swede's use Lingonberry sauce recipe on next page.

Lingonberry sauce

Total time: 18 minutes

Servings	12
Yield	3 cups

Ingredients

4 cups lingonberries
1⁄2 cup water
1 cup sugar

Directions

Drain berries, wash and pick out any leaves.
Place berries in saucepan; add water and heat to boiling.
Add sugar; stir to dissolve. Simmer 10 minutes.
Remove from heat.
Place saucepan in cold water; stir sauce for 1-2 minutes.
Serve warm if using for pancakes, chill if serving with meat.

Reindeer Stew

Total time: 2 hours
Servings 5-6

Ingredients

1 ½ lbs. bottom round beef roast (2 ¼ lbs. if using bone-in)
or 1 ½ lbs. elk roast (2 ¼ lbs. if using bone-in)
or 1 ½ lbs. reindeer meat, cut into 1-inch cubes (2 ¼ lbs. if using bone-in)

3 tablespoons flour
2 1/2 teaspoons salt
1 tablespoons butter
1 tablespoons olive oil
2 onions, cut into wedges
10 whole allspice or 2 teaspoons ground allspice

Directions

Coat the beef with flour and salt.
In a large, heavy pot melt the butter.
Sauté the meat until browned on all sides.
Add the onions and sauté for a few minutes with the meat.
Add allspice, bay leaves, and water, and stir well, scraping the sides and bottom of the pan well.
Add carrots, cover, and allow to simmer over low heat until meat is tender (1-1 ½ hours).
Stir occasionally to keep from sticking, and if needed, add more water.
Add potatoes, and return to boiling; cook until potatoes are tender (1/2 hour).

Rulltårta

Total time: 12-15 minutes

Ingredients

1 cup sifted cake flour	1 tsp. baking powder
2 Tbsp. butter	5 Tbsp. hot water
3 eggs	1 tsp. vanilla
¼ tsp. salt	1 cup gran. sugar
¼ cup powdered sugar	¾ cup jelly(any)

Directions

Heat oven to 375F

Grease a 15x10-inch baking pan. Line with wax paper; grease wax paper.

Mix flour and baking powder in a small bowl. Heat butter and water in a small saucepan on medium heat until butter is melted.

Beat eggs, vanilla, and salt in large bowl with electric mixer. Gradually add sugar, beating until thick and light in color. Gently stir in flour. Add butter mixture. Spread in prepared pan.

Bake 12-15 minutes.

Generously sprinkle cloth town with powdered sugar. Immediately turn cake out onto towel. Remove wax paper. Trim edges. Roll up cake in towel starting with short side. Cool completely on wire rack.

Unroll cake. Spread with jam. Re-roll.

Princesstarta
Swedish Princess Cake

****** These instructions seem very long drawn out but I assure you if you follow them to the T your princess cake will come out delicious******* ***Please read entire recipe before starting.***

Prep Time: 2 hours
Cook Time: 2 hours 5 minutes
Total Time: 4 hours 5 minutes
Yield: 20 servings

Ingredients
1 white cake mix   3 tbsp. raspberry jam

For Pastry Cream Filling:
2 cups half and half   5 egg yolks
3 tbsp. cornstarch   ½ cup sugar
pinch salt   1 tsp. vanilla
4 tbsp. cold unsalted butter, cut into small pieces

For Simple Syrup:
½ cup sugar   ½ cup water

For Whipped Cream:
3 cups heavy cream   3 tbsp. sugar
1 tbsp. vanilla

For Marzipan:
1 lb. Marzipan, store-bought or homemade
3 drops green food coloring
confectioner's sugar for dusting rolling pin

Directions

The day before assembling cake: Make the pastry cream: Bring the milk to a simmer in a large saucepan over medium-high heat. Whisk together the egg yolks, cornstarch, sugar, and salt in a bowl until smooth. Add half of the scalded milk into the bowl containing the eggs, constantly whisking to incorporate, then return the entire mixture to the saucepan containing the remaining milk, whisking over moderate heat. Continue whisking, about 2 to 5 minutes, until the mixture is thickened and begins to simmer. Allow pastry cream to a simmer, whisking for an additional 2 minutes. Remove from heat and whisk in vanilla and 4 tablespoons cold unsalted butter. Transfer into another bowl and allow to cool completely. Cover and refrigerate at least 5 hours and up to 3 days before using.

Prepare white cake mix per instructions, but pour 1/3 of batter into one 9" cake pan and 2/3 of batter into second 9" cake pan. Bake and cool on the rack. When cakes have cooled, use a serrated knife to slice the larger cake into two equal halves. (Note: cake can be prepared ahead of time and refrigerated, uncut, for 1 day or frozen, uncut, for up to a week. If baked ahead, slice the larger cake when assembling on the day of serving).

To assemble the cake (on the day of serving): Make a simple syrup by heating together 1 cup water and 1 cup sugar. Brush syrup lightly on each of the three cake layers, taking care not to oversoak.

For whipped cream, whip together 3 cups heavy cream, 3 tablespoon sugar, and 1 tablespoon vanilla until stiff peaks form.

For the marzipan: Knead green food coloring into

store-bought or homemade marzipan, then shape marzipan into an 8”-long disk. Place disk between two 18”-long lengths of waxed paper. Then, working from the middle of the marzipan, use a rolling pin to roll out the disk into a 16” circle of even thickness.

Spread 1 tablespoon raspberry jam on each of the two halves of the larger cake. Divide the pastry cream into thirds, folding 1/3 gently into the whipped cream. Spread the remaining 2/3 of the pastry cream on top of the raspberry jam level of the two cake halves. Stack the two pastry-covered halves, then top with the remaining cake.

Frost the sides of the cake with the whipped cream in a 1” layer, and then spoon the remaining whipped cream on top of the cake. Use a spatula to smooth the cream into a dome.

Remove the top level of waxed paper from the marzipan. Dust your rolling pin with confectioner’s sugar, then drape the marzipan circle over the pin and transfer it to the cake (you can lightly roll the marzipan around the pin as you would a pie crust).

With your hands, gently press the marzipan down over the cake, working from the top down. Smooth it down the sides, then cut off any excess at the bottom with a knife or cooking shears. Tuck in the marzipan under the edge of the cake. Tip: If the marzipan on the cake tears during placement, you can cut the remaining trimmings into decorative shapes and simply press these over the tears (this is a nice way to decorate the cake even if it’s perfect already! Alternatively, use additional uncolored or differently colored marzipan to create leaves, roses, or other shapes). Also: To hide less-than-perfect bottom edges, some bakers wrap a pretty ribbon around the bottom of the cake, removing before serving).

Sprinkle cake with confectioner’s sugar or decorate with marzipan cut-outs. Store in refrigerator for up to 1 week.

Raggmunks

Swedish Potato Pancakes

Total time: 25 minutes
Prep time: 5 minutes
Cook time: 20 minutes
Serving Size 25-30 pancakes

Ingredients
8 -10 slices thick bacon
6 medium potatoes (mealy potatoes grown in dry soil, like Idaho Russets)
1 cup milk
1 egg
2/3 cup all-purpose flour
2 teaspoons salt

Directions
Fry the bacon in large frying pan over medium heat until crisp, then transfer slices to paper towel to remove excess grease. Drain off all but 1 tablespoons of bacon fat from pan.
Whisk together the milk, egg, flour, and salt into a thin batter. Peel and then coarsely grate potatoes directly into batter. Stir to combine (Note: if batter seems thin, add additional flour in tablespoon increments until mixture holds together and is the consistency of thick yogurt).
Raise heat under frying pan to medium-high. Use a 1/4-cup measuring scoop to pour batter into small pancakes, about three inches in diameter; press each one lightly with spatula to spread thin and then fry quickly in bacon fat until golden, flipping once. Remove and place between sheets of paper toweling until ready to serve.
Serve with bacon and lingonberries.

www.ingramcontent.com/pod-product-compliance
Lightning Source LLC
Chambersburg PA
CBHW060538310726
48982CB00009B/1300/J

9780996561839